"Ah," he said contemp does not figure on your li

"Well, these last couple ~~ ~~~~ ~ ~~~~~~~ ~~~~ ~~~~ dark and handsome cannot feed me when I am hungry," Phoebe said philosophically, "or fix the leaking roof over my parent's head, unless of course he is handy with tools."

He grunted, "practicality over sentiment. Very unusual in a girl of your age."

"Ha," Phoebe snorted, "most women who rush into marriage never consider the practicality over the sentiment. People can't always live on love. Though I figure it helps when you are poor to like the person you are locked in poverty with."

Once more he threw back his head and laughed. "Phoebe... Phoebe...Phoebe. It is refreshing to hear your view on love. You have an honest view. Most women in my acquaintance will pretend that they love you, when all they love is the lifestyle. It's good when two people in a relationship can understand, from the get go, what they are in for."

UNHOLY MATRIMONY

BRENDA BARRETT

UNHOLY MATRIMONY
A Jamaica Treasures Book/February 2013

Published by Jamaica Treasures
Kingston, Jamaica

This is a work of fiction. Names, characters, places, and incidents are either the product of the author's imagination or are used fictitiously. Any resemblance to an actual person or persons, living or dead, events, or locales is entirely coincidental.

ISBN - 978-976-95566-2-1
Jamaica Treasures Ltd.
P.O. Box 482
Kingston 19
Jamaica W.I.
www.fiwibooks.com

Dear Reader

I really enjoyed writing the various characters in the Three Rivers Series. The series is set in Three Rivers, St. Ann, a little fictional town in Jamaica that is situated close to the famous Ocho Rios with its white sand beaches, verdant green mountains and lovely flowers.

The series starts out with Kelly, the pastor's wife, whose extra marital affair had far reaching consequences.

The second book in the series is about her sister, Erica, who is actively looking for a husband and had all but given up until she met the mysterious Caleb Wright who seemed to appear out of nowhere and had secrets he was afraid of sharing.

The third book is about Phoebe—whose main goal is to marry rich—she is forced to choose between Ezekiel who is rich but ugly, and Charles who is poor but handsome.

The final book in the series is about Chris who finds himself mysteriously drawn to his unsophisticated and opinionated housekeeper, while he battles the feelings he still harbors for Kelly.

Please, enjoy reading …

Yours Sincerely

Brenda Barrett

ALSO BY BRENDA BARRETT

ABOUT THE AUTHOR

Books have always been a big part of life for Jamaican born Brenda Barrett, she reports that she gets withdrawal symptoms if she does not consume at least two books per week. That is all she can manage these days, as her days are filled with writing, a natural progression from her love of reading. Currently, Brenda has several novels on the market, she writes predominantly in the historical fiction, Christian fiction, comedy and romance genres.

Apart from writing fictional books, Brenda writes for her blogs blackhair101.com; where she gives hair care tips and fiwibooks.com, where she shares about her writing life.

You can connect with Brenda online at:
Brenda-Barrett.com
Twitter.com/AuthorWriterBB
Facebook.com/AuthorBrendaBarrett

Chapter One

Phoebe sat in the front pew of the church for the wedding ceremony and tried to look pleasant. Erica had not let the dust settle under her feet after Caleb had proposed to her in front of everyone at church.

Her friend had gone into a mad flurry of excitement and had started planning her wedding that same night. She had declared that she wanted a church wedding at twilight on a Saturday and that she wanted the whole church to attend. No invitation was necessary and none was given. Erica had posted the date on the notice board with a cheekily written invitation to a chocolate fondue reception to follow the service.

Phoebe looked behind her, noting that the church was packed to the hilt. In a bid to make up for their insinuations about Caleb, the ladies of the church had outdone themselves with the decorations. Erica had requested a chocolate and burnt orange theme with hints of gold and they had gone all out. Some even wore the same colors to coordinate with the theme.

Even Phoebe had made an effort to coordinate her outfit too and she had haggled over the gold dress she was wearing with a store clerk who was reserving it for 'that rich lady Hyacinth Donahue.'

Phoebe had almost had a fit to get it and was again reminded why rich people were better off than the poor masses. She had finally gotten the dress, and had counted it a bittersweet victory.

Once again she had vowed that one day, they would all be chasing her to buy their merchandise and she would shun them. Oh, how she would shun them.

The junior orchestra was playing as Erica glided up the aisle on her father's arm—in her mother's lace dress. She looked beautiful and so pleased, that for once, Phoebe felt a glimmer of happiness for someone who had the audacity to tie the knot before she did. Her happy feeling didn't last long though as Tanya leaned toward her and whispered.

"Isn't she gorgeous?"

Phoebe nodded, but her mood soon changed and she was once again gripped by a sudden onset of depression. When would she ever find a man who loved her as much as Caleb loved Erica? Or even as Pastor Theo loved Kelly?

They were sitting to the end of the same pew as Kelly, she was beaming, her hair was tied up in an elaborate chignon and she was dressed in a chocolate brown dress with a sprig of orange flower in the bodice—Theo was holding her hand as if they were newlyweds.

Phoebe noticed that they had not carried the baby; only the two older children were sitting beside their parents.

She sighed and Tanya looked at her, her brows raised. "It's

a wedding, cheer up!"

"I know," Phoebe whispered, "but it's just that Erica and I discovered Caleb. If I hadn't driven him away that could've been me up there—happy, and getting married."

Tanya chuckled. "He was poor at the time you discovered him, remember?"

Phoebe snorted, "but he's not poor now, is he?"

Tanya shrugged. "No he is not, but the best part of all of this for him is that he got a woman who loved him whether he was poor or not."

"What are you trying to say?" Phoebe whispered fiercely, "that I am a gold digger?"

Tanya murmured, "who the cap fits...now shut up. They are about to say their vows."

Phoebe felt like strangling Tanya, but she valiantly tried to tune her mind into the service. Erica declared her 'I do's' loudly and with confidence, and Caleb had a besotted smile on his face.

Pastor Brick, the attendant pastor declared, "wherefore they are no more twain, but one flesh. What therefore God hath joined together, let not man put asunder. I now declare you husband and wife. You may kiss your bride Mr. Wright."

The deed was done.

Phoebe watched as Caleb and Erica engaged in a deep kiss that had the congregation oohing and aahing.

Tanya looked at her and grinned. "Their honeymoon is going to be hot enough to burn."

"Shut up," Phoebe snapped.

"What's gotten into you?" Tanya's smile slipped. "Usually you are more fun to hang out with. You know if you could only let go of your prejudices toward men, you would find someone."

"Argh," Phoebe growled, then forced a smile on her face

as the bride and groom turned to the congregation. "You don't know what you are talking about."

Tanya was clapping with the rest of the congregation and said to Phoebe sideways, "we'll pick this up at the reception in the church hall. Erica said she had more chocolate treats prepared than a chocolate shop."

Phoebe got up reluctantly when the usher indicated to her row first. She traipsed behind Tanya obediently and went to the door to congratulate Erica.

"Pheebs," Erica squealed when she saw her friend, "you wouldn't believe what Daddy and Mommy gave us as a wedding present?"

"What?" Phoebe asked injecting a note of excitement in her voice.

"We are going to Paris!" Erica squealed.

"Just for two weeks," Caleb said beside her.

"That's lovely!" Phoebe exclaimed. "I wish you all the best for the future and I am so happy for you."

Erica giggled. "Thank you my dear, I hope you find your Mr. Right soon."

Phoebe moved on, as there was a crush behind her to congratulate the effervescent bride. She walked out into the night air and spotted Tanya who was waving to her.

"As I was saying," Tanya said when she drew near, "you need to lower your expectations a little bit."

"Never," Phoebe said, a steely finality in her voice. "There must be a tall, dark, handsome, rich man in the world for me."

Tanya laughed. "There is. He's in your dreams, so dream on."

Phoebe looked over at the crowd with a sad feeling in the pit of her stomach. Maybe she really was aiming too high; maybe she was too picky and unrealistic. But oh, how sweet it would be to go for a honeymoon somewhere far away like Erica was, without pinching pennies.

"What about that guy Charles Black—your neighbor?" Tanya asked interestedly, intruding on her thoughts. "He is really good-looking."

"Poor," Phoebe snorted. "I don't even know what he does for a living."

Tanya giggled, "what about Ezekiel Hoppings? The rich ugly guy?"

"I gave him my number when I saw him at church last week." Phoebe responded sullenly.

Tanya choked back a laugh and then erupted, "are you serious? Are you really serious? The beautiful Phoebe Bridge, who will not tolerate imperfection in anyone, gave her number to that unfortunate looking man?"

Phoebe shuddered. "I did. He asked 'is it okay for me to call you sometime?' I said yes. End of story. He hasn't called since and I didn't take his number. So there—that's the end of that."

Tanya shook her head in awe, "I am sorry I dared to lecture you Pheebs. If you can consider Ezekiel Hoppings as a date, no matter how rich he is, I will say your standards of perfection are well and truly lowered. Let's go have some of those delectable chocolate desserts, the groom made, that Erica has been harping on about all week."

Chapter Two

Tanya gave Phoebe a lift to the low-income housing scheme where she lived. She waved as Tanya turned her car around, tooted her and drove off. Phoebe could smell a strong pungent pig scent as she had entered her street, and it was especially strong where she lived because her neighbor, on the right, reared pigs. His pigpen was especially smelly in the nights, and to make matters worse, her room was on the side of the house in the 'line of scent' to the pen.

She looked balefully at the house where she lived with her parents. Her mother had left on a light on the verandah and it showed up the ugly orange color that her father had painted it in. The paint had been leftovers from a job he had been doing at the time so he had dabbled the verandah with a single coat of the ugly color. It was peeling at some spots and little flecks of the orange paint were constantly shedding onto the extremely tiny verandah, which featured a run down wicker chair with a dirty cushion in it.

Phoebe fought a grimace when she approached her verandah and tried valiantly to shake the revulsion she always felt when she entered the yard with its dried up grass and a lone scraggly-looking orange tree.

Even in a neighborhood of modest houses and yards her family's house was obviously the worst looking. She had given up trying to spruce up the place. The last time she had splurged and used her paycheck to buy new glass windows, they broke during installation. Her father had shaken his head in resignation and boarded up the front windows with ply board, making the inside of the house was even darker and dingier than it was before. Phoebe entered through the front door, passed the small living room with the ugly red velvet settees and headed for the kitchen.

She placed the bag of chocolates she was clutching and put it on the counter space that was jammed in a small corner of the room—the Formica top was chipped and peeling in places.

Her mother, Nishta, was washing dishes and grunted a hello when she saw Phoebe.

Nishta Bridge was a pessimist with a defeatist attitude. She delighted in bad news and was constantly predicting dire results from all the major happenings in the world. She was also a conspiracy theorist who just loved to hear a hint of scandal to confirm her views that the world was descending into madness, just as she had predicted.

Her idea of entertainment was reading the death section of the national newspaper and connecting face and names with the news reports.

Phoebe could see that her mother had been a beauty in the past but her beauty was severely fading. Burdened with stress and anxiety over her living situation, Nishta appeared tired and took absolutely no pride in her appearance.

Her long coal-black hair was generously peppered with white streaks; she wore it caught up in a ponytail everyday. Though her honey-toned skin was smooth, she had two permanent worry lines etched between her eyes.

Nishta Bridge was just forty-nine but she looked at least ten years older. She had given up on diet and exercise and had gotten soft around the middle. She had two rolls of fat around her mid-section, and one roll around her neck. Her mouth was turned down in a permanent look of disapproval.

Phoebe looked into the pot and saw that she had cooked rice porridge for dinner. She screwed up her face in displeasure and closed the pot hurriedly.

"These are for you," Phoebe said indicating to the chocolates that she had gotten as souvenirs at Erica's wedding. "It was a really nice wedding, very romantic. Erica looked pretty in her white lace dress and the groom was gorgeous—they are going to Paris for their honeymoon."

"That's nice," Nishta mumbled. "Imagine that! Paris, the land of lovers," she sighed. "If only you could find a rich man and get married, you could honeymoon in exotic locales too. You could even take us out of our misery."

She looked at Phoebe, her brown eyes tearing up. "You are getting old Phoebe. When I was your age I was long married. If I had not picked such a poor man like your father, life would be so much different for me. At least I could eat well every night instead of having porridge or whatever measly food your father provides. By the way," she flashed her soapy hands and grabbed a towel, "the money you spent on that dress you are wearing could feed us for at least five nights this week."

Phoebe leaned onto the wall and patiently listened to her mother as she bemoaned their poverty and how she was the only hope. The talk was always the same and Phoebe feverishly wondered when she could politely retire to her room or better yet, escape this house.

"Can you imagine what life would be like if we were rich, Phoebe girl? We could live like queens, go on one of those cruises that I see them advertising on television. Except we would be going on our own yacht, cruising around the Caribbean, stopping at whatever port would catch our fancy."

"It would be nice wouldn't it?" Phoebe asked, allowing herself to dare to dream like her mother—her mother always managed to pull her into her delusions of grandeur. There was a time when she would resist, but not tonight.

Tonight she was especially keyed up from seeing Erica getting married and she wanted somebody to talk to, even if that person had a one-track mind about riches and marriage.

Nishta leaned on the counter and looked at Phoebe, her eyes alight. "We could stay in any fancy hotel when we feel like it, or we could live like the Donahues in a lovely house overlooking the bay area. I was so disappointed when you didn't get that handsome Chris Donahue to like you back. Some men are so blind. You are beautiful; you have a lovely shape and a truly gorgeous face. What was the matter with that man?"

"Don't start that again Mama," Phoebe said taking the pins from her hair and moving out to the sitting room— her mother's favorite topic was the Donahues and how rich they were. A few years ago she had pushed Phoebe to pursue Chris Donahue, to the extent that he had publicly announced in church that he wasn't interested in her and had even gone as far as to take out a restraining order against her.

The humiliation was one she had buried under her list of things not to think about too much. She had appeared to the world as if she didn't care, but the whole experience had hurt her deeply. After the devastating put down at church she had come home the night and had bawled like a baby.

She hadn't even really liked Chris anyway, but her mother had waged a marriage campaign with him as the centerpiece—it had backfired horrendously.

"Where's Dad?" she asked her mother who was rummaging through the bag of chocolates and regarding each candy with worshipful devotion.

"He is laid up in bed," Nishta grunted. "His back gave way this evening, which means he'll not be able to work for the next couple of weeks. Which means porridge for dinner for the rest of the week."

Phoebe shrugged. Her father was periodically out of a job; this was nothing new. He was a seasonal worker and usually got odd jobs around town, usually in construction until whatever he had planted on his farm came to fruition. For most of her childhood she could recall being hungry for days when he was out of a job. Luckily, she had gotten a job at the bank and was now able to care for the three of them until he could start working again.

Her mother was a housewife who never worked a day in her life, and had never even completed high school. Nishta's parents had never seen the need for it. They thought that girls had one use, and that was to take care of their husband's house.

They had arrived in Jamaica, from India, with some very archaic ideas for their four girls; her mother had been the youngest and the most brainwashed.

She had also been the only one who dared to court a non-Indian. They had taken her defiance very hard and after several warnings, a defiant Nishta was kicked out of her parent's house with nothing but the clothes on her back.

Out of necessity she had ended up marrying Larry Bridge, a poor struggling farmer who had not been ready for marriage. By the time Phoebe arrived on the scene, after five miscarriages, her parents had been locked into a partnership with poverty.

They had lived in a one-room shack on Larry's one-acre farmland and for most of Phoebe's life, up until age twelve, there they had remained, until some kind Samaritan had signed up Larry for affordable housing in a low-income housing scheme. He had gotten one of the two bedroom houses on a small square of land.

Through the years, their poverty hadn't changed much and before Phoebe could do algebra, or even memorize a Bible verse her mother had only one counsel—never marry poor.

It was a mortal sin to marry poor.

It was a chorus Phoebe knew well, and while she sat in the small settee in the dingy living room she found herself wondering about Ezekiel Hoppings. She had declined to mention him to her mother; she was in no mood for a one of her mother's battle plan to woo Ezekiel. Besides, the man was so far out of their class that he was in another stratosphere. And he was ugly. He had the face only a mother could love and no matter how many times Phoebe tried to tell herself that all that mattered was the lifestyle she would have after she got married, she felt a mild aversion to even think about Ezekiel that way. She could not imagine waking up in the mornings to Ezekiel's face or to sit facing him at the dining table night after night.

She glanced around her at the dust covered center table with a five-week-old newspaper sprawled in the middle and the pale pink curtains her mother had gotten at a bargain store and shuddered.

Did it truly matter how a person looked when they had enough money to dig her out of her mire of poverty?

She was twenty-four, as her mother kept reminding her,

her good looking days were numbered. Next year she would be twenty-five, time was running out on her.

At seventeen her mother had entered her in a beauty contest and she had placed third. The other two girls had rich fathers and had been placed in the top spots because of their daddy's connections. Phoebe's mother had never ventured to suggest any more contests after that. To Nishta, being rich even trumped being beautiful, the contest had cemented that in her mind even more.

At eighteen, Phoebe had seen one beauty queen after the other being propelled into the spotlight and she had become convinced that beauty contests were the only way to become popular and to bag herself a rich husband. It was the only way she could foresee that she could meet the right sort of people but her father had chosen that time to put his foot down about modesty and chastity.

'No child of mine will parade on a stage half dressed to be judged like a heifer.'

Phoebe rolled her eyes; if she had had the money then she would have done it, no matter what her father said. His Christianity was as seasonal as his jobs, and he always found the most inappropriate time to demonstrate it.

These days he hardly came to church and when he did, he always managed to embarrass her by testifying about how poor he was but he was happy that God had blessed him with a beautiful daughter. His simple, child-like ways were always a source of discontent for her and she was always trying to disassociate herself from him.

She tried really hard to be normal with the church people, but she didn't appreciate her less than stellar background being paraded around by her father in his heartfelt testimonies that were always filled with too much information about their life.

She sometimes wondered if God v
her— why he made her with such a b
in such a poor family. What lesson ᴗ

It was a puzzle to her—every pretty ɡ.
either pampered and happy, or pampered and riᴄ.

She looked at her mother, who was wiping dowᴎ
kitchen counter after stuffing all the chocolate delicacies into
her mouth.

Her sighs of despair were loud enough for Phoebe to hear
and the sense of unease that she always felt when she heard
her mother's distress was creeping upon her again.

It was a combination of guilt and gloom. She suddenly
wished she had gotten Ezekiel Hoppings' number. She would
willingly sacrifice all she had not to feel this way anymore,
even feigning an interest in 'the ugliest man in the world.'

She grimaced at the thought, "I am going to bed Ma," she
said heading to her room.

"Sleep well," Nishta said a heaviness to her voice. She
barely glanced at Phoebe and continued wiping down the
counter dejectedly.

Chapter Three

Phoebe woke up Sunday morning and stared at her water stained ceiling. She did her usual morning exercise of trying to make out the patterns created in the ceiling. This morning she could make out the shape of a man who was around a desk typing, and a lady in a ballerina dress. The extremely brown areas, where the water had settled on the ceiling, were widening by the day. It was one more thing on her list of house repairs to do and she was tired of it. Maybe one day she would wake up and find that the untidy ramshackle place she called home had crumbled around her while she slept.

Her father had promised to repair the roof last week but that had been pushed back when he got a job—finally. Now that he was injured she didn't know when he would be fit again to tackle the roof.

Maybe never.

Earlier in the morning, she had heard him singing a song and then praying loudly. She had wanted to join him but she had cynically thought that his Christianity was back on and she wanted no part of it this time. When he was injured he was usually quite fervent about God and when he was healthy God usually took a back seat to work. Through the paper thin walls of the house Phoebe could hear him bribing God with promises of how faithful he would be when his back was straightened out again.

She laughed inwardly, her mother was an ardent non-Christian and yet, even in her stubborn reticence, struck Phoebe as the more genuine parent in her attitude to God. Her mother had given up on God a long time ago and usually ignored her husband when he was fervent about praying. Only poor people love God, was her mother's reasoning, and nothing Phoebe said could convince her otherwise.

She had almost convinced Phoebe of the same, but by then, she had genuinely loved going to the Three Rivers Church. The young people had incorporated her into their club and so she hadn't cared what her mother had to say about God at that time.

She had proudly gone to church alone, year after year, even while her mother hemmed and hawed that 'your fascination with this church business is the reason why we are not rich', Nishta would murmur, 'let down your standards a bit, wear some tighter clothes, you have nice legs flash them. You need to smile more and let others see those lovely white teeth. Rich men are as scarce as hen's teeth in church, start going to some of those clubs like Rotary and Kiwanis.'

Phoebe sighed and dragged herself out of bed faster than she normally did on a Sunday morning, but the pigpen scent had her shallowly gasping and contemplating the day ahead. She wished she had somewhere to go to escape the house and its fetid stench.

She had tried reasoning with Mr. Roberts, her next-door

neighbor, about the unpleasantness of the smell that the people in the neighborhood were subjected to, but he had laughed at her, patted her hand and called her a 'pretty little thing.'

The price for pigs was increasing every day and he had no intention of selling his pigs until he could fetch a premium for them. He also had no intention of cleaning the pen. Since he was immune to the stench in his backyard he figured everybody should be too.

She pulled on a faded red blouse and a cut off shorts with paint splatters and went outside—her glowing caramel skin and wavy hair, as usual, had men slowing down and whistling as they passed the house.

Phoebe leaned on the rusty gate, with a far away look in her eyes. She usually ignored her neighbors, and they took her attitude as haughty disdain for them but Phoebe wasn't in the mood to care right now. She felt too discontent and unhappy.

She barely registered when the sound of a sputtering bike drew up at the gate beside hers, until Charles Black cleared his throat loudly.

"If it isn't Miss Phoebe."

Phoebe glanced over at him and smirked. "If it isn't the idle guy who lives next door."

Charles laughed and took off his biker's helmet. He was dressed in a red shirt that highlighted his dark caramel skin tone. He was quite handsome: with a tall, leanly muscled physique and dusky pink lips. His hair was cut in a Mohawk style and he had a designer goatee thing going.

Charles paused before he approached Phoebe at her gate. Usually he was pretty irresistible to women, but since he moved next door to the Bridge's, six months ago, he had been trying to get Phoebe's attention, to no avail. She looked through him as if he was invisible, and it was enough to give a guy a complex.

He spent days trying to work out in his mind how he would get Phoebe to like him. He considered lying in front of her gate and begging her to pay him some attention but he feared she would just step on him as she went on her way.

Yesterday he had gathered enough courage to introduce himself to her while she was hanging out her underclothes on the clothesline at the back of the house. He had popped his head over the fence and surprised her, but she had given him a look of such pure hatred that he had wondered if he had done her something wrong that he knew nothing about.

Charles walked over to stand in front of the gate that Phoebe was leaning on and almost felt tongue tied when he gazed at her. She was even more beautiful close up. Her creamy honey complexion, the symmetry of her features, the curly tendrils of her hair, all culminated in quite a beautiful package.

He mustered some of the courage that he had developed from working with people for years as a tour guide at the Mayfield Falls, to face the most beautiful forbidding woman he had ever tried to engage in conversation.

He crossed his arms in a relaxed stance and grinned at her. "I know you know what my name is, Phoebe Bridge. I saw you hanging out your panties just yesterday morning and I introduced myself."

Phoebe gasped. "You are so crass and uncouth."

Charles laughed, his deep brown eyes, lighting up with mirth, "I'm not sure what you just called me but it sounds wonderful. You are the most beautiful girl I have ever seen and the words from your mouth are like music to my ears."

Phoebe kissed her teeth. "Sweet talk from a poor guy who rides a bike—not interested."

Charles cleared his throat and grinned cheekily. "I will have you know that I got a job at the Hotel Flamingo as an entertainment coordinator. I might be able to afford a bigger bike by next year."

Phoebe closed her eyes and sighed. "As I said, not interested."

Charles' smile slowly disappeared. "I play in a band."

Phoebe turned around to leave.

"I play piano at church and sometimes guitar," Charles said frantically. "You know the church—Great Pond. I saw you there when I just moved here...saw you there with a friend one night. That was my very first concert."

Phoebe looked back at him. "Congrats. Keep on playing your music."

Charles moved closer to the gate. "I also play for weddings and other social occasions. In fact, we are playing at a party in Bluffs Head tonight," he said, talking faster now as he watched Phoebe's retreating back. "It is supposed to be some super-exclusive thing. One of our band members is sick; so you could come in his place."

Phoebe slowed down and looked back at him. "Did you say Bluffs Head? Where the richest of the rich people live?"

Charles nodded earnestly. She was actually talking to him. "Yeah, you could come. They are expecting seven of us. I could take you in place of Brad, they won't know the difference and you could attend a nice party. I won't be able to talk to you much though since we'll be playing most of the time...my friend Darren won't mind. He is the one who set up the gig and is the band leader."

Phoebe advanced closer to the gate, her mind ticking overtime. Bluffs Head was seriously exclusive. The only people who found themselves up there were the rich, and the service people who tended to them.

If she could just get a taste of that lifestyle, see how they lived, rub shoulders with the best of them, or find herself a rich guy who would be interested in her. It was perfect.

She looked at Charles with renewed energy. "I'll come. What sort of party is it?"

"Uh...er...I guess elegant." Charles stuttered. Phoebe was smiling at him benignly and he suddenly felt blessed. Like he had been conferred a great honor by a queen.

"Okay..." she could probably wear that black slip dress that she had been saving for ages to go somewhere nice, she thought to herself, and then looked at Charles again, a beatific smile spreading over her face as she thought about the evening ahead. "What time should I be ready?"

"About five," Charles said relieved that he had found the key to having Phoebe talk to him. "We have to set up, do mike checks, that sort of thing...the party starts at seven."

"So I'll have to come and sit around?" Phoebe asked suddenly put off. She could just loudly state that she was a service person then. Nobody would mistake her for a guest.

Charles' smile deflated. "Setting up is still fun."

Phoebe frowned and then finally she sighed. Who was she kidding? Here was her only chance to see the inside of a Bluffs Head mansion, and she was put off by going there too early? She must be mad to even think of turning down this wonderful opportunity.

"I'll be ready."

"Can I get your number to call you in case of anything?" Charles asked trying to keep a casual look on his face before Phoebe figured out that he was jumping for joy inside.

"Oh sure," Phoebe said and gave it to him without a thought. She was so caught up in the possibilities of the night that she hadn't even registered that Charles was still leaning on the gate with a puppy dog look in his eyes while she headed inside the house.

Chapter Four

Phoebe mumbled the whole way to Bluffs Head. It turned out that the black slip dress that she had hoped to wear had several white spots on the front and looked like a polka dot horror—her mother had accidentally ruined it with bleach. It would have been perfect to wear to an elegant party, and sophisticated enough to make her fit in.

Instead, she had to settle for a red velvet textured dress that shouted low income. She was in the process of tugging down the hem when she looked up to see five pairs of eyes watching her intently.

She had chosen to sit in the very back of Darren's bus to avoid sitting beside any of the guys. She had jammed herself beside a guitar and a box with long cords coiled up in it. The bus smelled like bubblegum.

The eyes were still regarding her with interest.

"Shouldn't you be facing forward?" she asked them while she struggled to sit straight as the bus took a sharp corner.

"Is she real?" one of them asked Charles, completely ignoring Phoebe's question and looking at her awestruck.

"Yes," Charles said gleefully. He was wearing a red satin shirt and black pants like the rest of them and Phoebe suddenly realized she was in red too, the exact shade of red that they were wearing.

She groaned, "I feel like Gladys Knight with the Pips."

"Our band is called the The Perfect Number." One of them said, his eyes fastened on her steadily. "We are usually seven guys but Brad got food poisoning from eating oranges. Can you believe it?" He laughed nervously and made a honking sound.

Phoebe closed her eyes and tried to ignore them. She didn't even remember their names. Charles had introduced them when he had stopped at her gate, promptly at five, but all she heard was Happy, Sleepy, Sleazy, Grumpy, Dopey, she already knew Charles and the one driving was Darren.

When she opened her eyes again, Sleazy asked Charles, "are those her real breasts?"

"Forget that," Dopey said, "are those eyelashes real?"

"Stop acting like you've never seen a girl before," Charles said to his friends in frustration.

"Never seen one like this," Grumpy said, "except in music videos and magazines. Is she photo-shopped?"

Charles sighed. "Garwin, shut up. She's real."

"And lives beside you?" Dopey asked incredulously, "in Flatbush Scheme?"

Phoebe couldn't wait to get to the party, and pretend like she didn't know them.

The vehicle was climbing the hill and advancing through a middle class neighborhood. The houses were well kept and the lawns manicured. Phoebe couldn't help but notice how much the view improved and the land space between the houses widened the further they went up the hill.

They passed an imposing mansion, which had exquisite cut stonework on the front and some beautiful flowers in the yard.

"Wow," Phoebe said totally impressed.

"That's Chris Donahue's house," Charles said enjoying the fact that Phoebe was impressed with their date so far, even though he had nothing to do with it. "He goes to your church."

"It's nice," Phoebe said struggling to close her mouth and act blasé.

Charles laughed, the others giggled too and then Phoebe realized that they had stopped at a gate. The imposing wrought iron gate had a security booth at the front. On a nameplate in the stout cut stonewall, was the name Lion's Head.

Wasn't this the mansion Erica said belonged to Ezekiel Hoppings? She hadn't been able to see from the road what the house looked like when she had coerced Erica to drive by, just a few short months earlier.

Was she gate crashing Ezekiel's party? What if he recognized her?

Phoebe felt a shaft of fear grip her. She couldn't stand embarrassment. She couldn't deal with the humiliation of being called out as a poor imposter who had to resort to pretending to be a service person to attend a high-class party. She wanted to go back home. Her confidence had taken off down the hill and she wanted to run after it.

"Step out of the vehicle please." The security guards surrounded the van as if prisoners were in it and everybody filed out of the vehicle. A pink-faced Phoebe followed behind Charles.

"Who is she?" one especially fierce looking guard asked

when Phoebe stood a little behind the boys. His name was Bryan; she could see it on his ID, which was clipped to his shirt pocket.

"She is...she...er..." Darren was stuttering like he was guilty of something.

"She is replacing Bradley on the list," Charles piped up to help his friend.

The security looked hard at her like she was a criminal.

"State your name, occupation and address on this paper." He shoved a piece of paper, under Phoebe's nose.

Phoebe felt so humiliated. When had anybody been treated with such cold disregard before entering a party?

She scratched down her information, her hands trembling.

The security took the paper from her and glanced over it; another security went into the van with an instrument and another searched the van thoroughly. There were four of them, all of them massive, and serious-looking. One of them ran a scanning device over the group members one-by-one and then stepped back. Another returned with her red purse and handed it to her.

"Please open your bag Miss so that we can verify that its contents aren't contraband."

"Contra...contraband?"

The security didn't even nod; he gazed at her coldly.

Phoebe opened her purse; they glanced at her phone, her lipstick and a pack of gum and then nodded.

"You need to give us the phone."

"But...but why."

The taller security standing behind him smiled with an even scarier look than his serious expression and said gruffly, "we do not allow instruments on the compound that can take unauthorized pictures and videos. That was on the list of rules for the service people. You should have told your friend here." He said looking at the boys who were awestruck and looking on the security slightly fearfully.

Charles muttered, "sorry Phoebe."

He took Phoebe's phone and said, "when you are leaving you will get it back. I also took your recorder," he said staring at the guys, "when you are leaving you will get it back too."

He waved them on, "have a nice party."

The four of them once more took up defensive poses as they all trooped back into the van and watched the iron gate slowly open for them. Phoebe's dreams of waltzing into the party, as a much revered beautiful woman, died a slow painful death as she sat down and heard her red dress make a ripping sound.

*****

It was a tear to the side. She had picked off the hanging threads and hoped against hope that it wouldn't split all the way up to her armpit. She wished she had a safety pin to secure the ragged edges, but she was out of luck and even if she did have one, those security men would have probably confiscated it as a weapon of mass destruction.

Phoebe sat at the far end of the pool area and tried to ignore the curious stares she was getting from the people who were setting up tables on the other side. The place was too imposing for words. When they drove up to the parking lot, which was surrounded by colorful miniature trees, they were lead by a security guard, who was wearing a tux, to the pool area.

The back of the house had steps leading down a rocky incline to the sea. Then there was an infinity pool, which started from the marble steps of a gazebo and meandered toward the edge of an area with big slabs of polished stone.

She wished she had a camera, nobody would believe her if she described to them the luxury that she was seeing.

Phoebe had never seen such a display of wealth in her life. She walked around the vast pool area and then found herself a corner which had strategically placed sofas scattered between lanterns and cleverly placed mini-trees to ensure privacy.

The Perfect Number was not the only band playing; she counted at least three other groups that looked as if they were in costume. They were also busy setting up. One usher had given her a program, which she hadn't even glanced at yet.

I could get used to this, Phoebe decided. This could be all hers if she wanted. She couldn't believe how shortsighted and stupid she had been when it came to Ezekiel. She could picture herself driving up the long tree-lined driveway in a high-end car and swimming in the infinity pool on a hot afternoon, or having somebody come up to the house to do her nails. Or she could get a massage by the beach side below.

If she hung over the protective rail, to the side, she could see the white sand just below the steps, in what looked like a protected cove with hulking gray rocks all around.

She was brought out of her reverie when a lady appeared to the right of her.

"Shouldn't you be practicing with your band?" The lady asked sharply.

"Uhm..." Phoebe looked around her to the far end, there was another group doing mike tests but Charles' band was nowhere to be seen. "I would but they are not around."

The lady who was in an elegant green dress, which matched the green baubles around her neck, sat down in the seat across from Phoebe and sighed. Her hair was a light brown which matched her eyes perfectly. She looked to be in her late thirties.

She was also assessing Phoebe and they stared at each other before the lady spoke. "You weren't invited to this party."

Phoebe shrugged. "What's it to you?"

"I am the hostess of the party. My name is Sonia Beaumont."

"Oh sorry," Phoebe said slightly shocked. "I thought this was Ezekiel's place."

"Ezekiel!" the lady closed her eyes as if in pain. "You are calling such a respectable man, a man way out of your league, Ezekiel."

Phoebe shrugged, "how respectable is he?"

"Do you have any idea who I am?" the lady asked a flash of indignant light in her eyes.

"Nope," Phoebe said staring at her fascinated, "should I?"

"I am the person who forced him to have this party, I am the one who organized this shindig. I said to him 'Ezekiel you are too insular, your presence needs to be felt in this community, after all Jamaica is your home for five months of the year.' He finally agreed. I invited the top industry movers and shakers on the island, fellow rich people and you know what, not a reaction. Then he sees your name, sent in by the security detail at the gate, and suddenly he is happy. Maybe, I should have invited all the low-income residents of Flatbush Scheme!"

She got up, "I would have had you thrown out by the way," she mumbled. "I know your type and let me tell you something, you are no match for me. Did you hear that?" Sonia asked her grimly before she stormed off, her dress bellowing in the breeze.

Phoebe nodded, though she wanted to smirk at Sonia. What was she getting so worked up over? She didn't know if she should laugh or cry. So, Ezekiel knows I'm here and is happy about it? And this lady was actually warning her

off Ezekiel, a man she had hardly spoken two words to—
usually when he saw her at church he stared at her fixatedly
while she tried to pretend that she didn't see him looking.

The delicious irony of it.

Phoebe looked at her, a new light of knowledge in her eyes,
here she was feeling trodden and out-of-place and singled
out for a warning from a high-class lady.

Phoebe had never been docile in her entire life and was a
fighter; this lady just declared war. She didn't care much for
the prize because he was ugly, but he was also wealthy and
Phoebe wasn't going to lose this war for the affections of
Ezekiel Hoppings. She just needed a battle plan.

Chapter Five

Ezekiel eagerly shrugged on his tuxedo. He had not wanted a party but Sonia had insisted. She had appointed herself 'caretaker of his property' and because he was a friend of her brother he had allowed her to run his household as if she was its mistress.

He had gradually come to realize, on this trip to Jamaica, that Sonia had plans for him to marry her. She was touching him more and sidling up to him when he was seated with an eager light of warmth in her eyes.

He should·be pleased with the turn of events, he knew. Sonia was thirty-nine, a recent divorcee with two young sons and was caring, a true mother earth type. She genuinely liked him and saw past his looks to the man beneath.

He had celebrated his fortieth birthday just a few weeks ago in an Abu Dubai boardroom with four Arab sheiks and his lawyers while he was there divesting his holdings in the Middle East. He wanted to do something else with his life and the cutthroat world of business didn't give him the zing it once did.

He was tired of flying to and from the Middle East, living out of expensive hotels, dealing with men who would much rather see him fail than see him succeed.

He wanted to live life at a slower pace. His father had been the ultimate tycoon, with holdings across the length and breadth of both hemispheres but had developed heart problems at forty-three.

The truth was, when he was younger, and more immature, he had thought that he wanted to be like his father—powerful and ruthless. He had taken some business risks in the last few years that would make ordinary men tremble. They called him the roaring lion in the Arab world, but these days he was feeling the ill effects of his fast paced lifestyle. He was now feeling his mortality— tired and worn-out, he found himself brooding and wanting a more moderately paced existence.

Ezekiel was tired of fighting. Life shouldn't be so adrenalin packed all the time. He stared at his reflection in the mirror and found himself wishing that he didn't have so much responsibility and thousands of people depending on him for their livelihood.

He sometimes wished that he was one of those ordinary men who went to work in the mornings, did an honest day and came back to a loving woman at nights who was attentive to his needs.

Instead he had been born with the proverbial gold spoon in his mouth, the oldest son to an Arab father who married an affluent Jamaican woman who had been living in Italy on her gap year from university.

He ran his fingers through his short curly hair and assessed his reflection in the mirror.

His body was leanly muscular, exercising was a daily habit

that he had picked up from rehab when he was seventeen and involved in the plane crash that killed his parents and his siblings.

He could rectify his face. His friend Neville Tate, one of the leading cosmetic surgeons in the world, was always hounding him about it but he had used his appearance to assess people for so long that he was reluctant to do anything to himself now. The people who could stick around, despite his scars, he usually kept close, those who were repulsed, he usually watched gleefully as they stayed far away from him, as if his scars were contagious.

When he did business, men looked at him and shuddered, they usually wondered how he earned his battle scars, and women usually looked at him and ran the other way. Through the years there were a few genuine ones who didn't seem to mind his looks, but he found that he hadn't captured that elusive feeling called love with any woman—until now.

He hadn't felt this maelstrom of feelings for any woman at any other time in his life. He felt curiously light, like he could float with the feeling of euphoria and then some days he felt down and depressed. His feelings were ping ponging all over the place like a tennis ball.

Ezekiel paced the room, anxious to go down to the poolside and meet with Phoebe Bridge. He was trying not to wonder about her. For months he had agonized over whether to pursue her. He had endured sleepless nights thinking about her and had to call upon his powers of self-control not to call her when she had given him her number.

There was something about that girl that was different from all the girls he had ever seen or known. It wasn't just her beauty, though one was constantly reminded of how utterly breathtaking she was. She had that indefinable quality that he felt as if he was searching for his whole life. It must be chemistry, it's as if all the pieces of his puzzle fell into place when she was near.

He had even had her investigated. There was very little that he didn't know about her, at least on paper.

He was astonished when the security detail had scanned in her name for approval just now. Sonia had been sitting with him in his study running through the boring guest list with him and he had sat in a comatose state half listening to her, half thinking that he was going to divest his holdings in Australia to reduce his traveling commitments.

But when the name Phoebe Bridge wafted over his consciousness his whole being had become alert, as if a switch had been turned on. She was in a bus at his gate, attending his party as a replacement for a band member.

He had almost laughed out loud at that—Phoebe was not a singer. He knew that about her, and why he should still remember these things was a puzzle to him.

What was it about her?

"Let her in," he had said to Sonia gruffly.

"But she is a crasher," Sonia had huffed.

"A beautiful crasher," he had sprung to his feet, "I need to get ready for this party."

"But she is from Flatbush Scheme," Sonia protested looking at the address on the computer screen. "That's the land settlement my father had developed for the poor farmers on the banana belt. She is a nobody, crashing my party."

Ezekiel had grinned, the scar along his cheekbone puckered in several creases. "You just spent half an hour convincing me to be excited about this party. Well, I'm excited now. Phoebe is here."

"Phoebe is here!" Sonia gasped. "You know this girl?"

"Yes, as a matter of fact I do, I have been going to her church for three years now. I always sit at the back. I leave quietly though. Trust me, when you see Phoebe you'll know, she's hard to miss."

Sonia had stormed out of the study and down to the pool area. He wondered what she had said to Phoebe.

The Phoebe that he researched would not care at all. She would probably sit there looking placidly about her as Sonia tried her best to put her down. Phoebe was a hard nut to crack.

He chuckled softly. He had seen her in action several times. He had even seen her being called out at church for stalking Chris Donahue. She had sat down, her dainty hands clenched together and a blank look on her face.

She had then proceeded to make the announcements that she had been assigned to make at the start of the church service, without any outward sign that she had been humiliated. It had been like water off a duck's back.

Yes he knew enough about Phoebe to know what he was letting himself in for. She was going to be a challenge if he pursued her.

She was a complex puzzle of strength and hardness but he could see that her strength could be masking a soft core. He wished he knew if she was as hardened by life as she appeared or if she was putting up a brave face to the world.

She was also fifteen years younger than he was and so beautiful. She was the beauty to his beast; he tried to remember how that fairytale turned out but couldn't.

He glanced at himself in the mirror again. He was not handsome. Scars crisscrossed his face and neck area and puckered skin ran across his forehead. His teeth had been yellowed by a heavy coffee diet while he was in his twenties. Though he had weaned himself from it, he still had the stains testifying to his former habit. His nose was broken in two places and looked off center; his skin was patchy with burn marks.

Normally he just accepted his looks for what they were, because he had developed a morbid fear of surgery but Phoebe's beauty highlighted his ugliness—he grimaced a little. If he succeeded in having her love him as he was, he would consider his life complete.

He was nervous. He could hear the music starting up downstairs. He glanced at his watch...quarter to seven; people were starting to mill about. It was time he went down and faced Phoebe.

Chapter Six

Phoebe watched from her cozy corner where she had partially hidden herself as the darkness descended and then the lights flickered on, the fancy lantern lamps lit up in various colors.

Where she sat was semi-dark and intimate. She could make out the shapes of people who were around the pool but could not see them clearly. The place was cleverly set up to appeal to the social butterflies or others who just wanted to chat in the dimly lit alcoves.

People had started to come in at six thirty. She could make out, from where she was, some government officials, a few industry leaders and that lady Sonia flitting in and out of the little groups, her laugh tinkling on the night air.

Phoebe cradled a fruit drink close to her, and watched silently. There were two waiters who had insisted on giving her the royal treatment and kept coming by to find out if she wanted little delicacies to eat and kept topping up her glass of juice. There was a lady sitting in the alcove next to hers, who had spent half an hour on her phone giving her babysitter instructions.

Then the music had started, Charles and his friends were really good. Charles played the keyboard and she could see his outline from where she sat, enthusiastically pounding the keys.

She had come all the way to a high-class party and was hiding in the background. Twice she had attempted to go into the fray but this crowd just didn't talk to you unless they knew you. She had stood around the food area and the women had looked through her as if she didn't exist and the men had given her a discrete once over and moved along. No one even said hello!

Not that she wanted them to anyway. Most of them were older and had big bellies and florid features. No young handsome upcoming man was in the crowd the last time she went out there. The only younger handsome men she saw were service people and she was not going to get embroiled in that.

"You look pensive." He sat in the chair opposite hers, his back was blocking out the light, but she could make out that he was tall and had on a tux.

"Not really pensive just bored." Phoebe said trying to peer into the darkness to make him out. He sounded like he had a slight English accent and smelled so good and expensive.

The man chuckled, "not your kind of crowd is it?"

He reclined in the chair besides hers and the leaves of the plant beside his head blotted out his facial profile.

"How'd you know that?" Phoebe asked suspiciously, trying to see him, she gave up in defeat as he angled his head closer to the plant in the opposite chair.

"You are sitting in the dark alone, cradling your fruit juice for dear life and you look like you feel left out."

"Well…" Phoebe debated telling him anything and then she gave in, she was really bored, she had wanted to leave about half an hour ago but she wasn't going to attempt walking downhill to the gate and then to the mercies of the dark streets to go home.

"I don't fit in with the crowd here at all. I only came because I was curious and my neighbor suggested it."

"Ah," he laughed softly, "you wanted to see how the other half lives."

"Well, I wouldn't call the rich population in Jamaica half." Phoebe said, reclining in her chair too, "I'd call it ten percent or so. By the way, who are you?"

"My name is Abbas," he said quietly.

"Abbas?" Phoebe asked, "strange name."

"It means Lion in the Arabian language," Abbas replied.

"Oh," Phoebe perked up, interested, "are you one of those rich Arabians who does business with Ezekiel Hoppings?"

"You could say that." His voice turned somber. "What is your name?" he asked after a long pause.

"Phoebe Bridge. My paternal grandmother's name was Phoebe, so I got her name. Apparently there is always a Phoebe Bridge on my Dad's side of the family."

"It is a great honor when one carries a name worthy to live up to." Abbas said almost lazily. "What do you do Phoebe Bridge?"

"Well, I work at a bank." Phoebe smirked. "I am a bank teller. I work specifically in customer service. It would be a nice job if one felt like being pleasant all the time but for me it's hell. What do you do?"

"I own companies all over the world," Abbas said softly. "I fly all over the world at the drop of a hat to places where people absolutely need my attention. My life is one crisis after another. Now that's hell. I am trying to scale down from my larger ventures and to stop and smell the roses."

"But you are rich right?" Phoebe asked eagerly, "how can that be hell?"

Abbas chuckled, "riches come with responsibility. My parents died when I was a teenager. I inherited oil wells, vineyards, oil production companies, and big world food brands. When my father's lawyers placed the folders before me that outlined the interests that my father had all over the world, I was literally paralyzed with fear. I was now the custodian of that legacy and it was a nightmare to sort out. He had heart problems at forty-three, I think that's where I am heading, if I don't take it easy. Unlike him, I have no offspring to leave anything to."

"Oh my," Phoebe said thinking about what he said for a minute, money did come with hard work and responsibility. She had only ever looked on the easy side and not really considering that it had to come from some effort on somebody's part.

"That's why I haven't married yet," Abbas said in the silence. "A wife could never live with my lifestyle. Most of my acquaintances in the business world are on their third wife by forty."

Phoebe cleared her throat; her heart skipped a beat in excitement. "So are you actively looking for a wife?"

Abbas laughed out loud, and Phoebe could see him throwing back his head in the lounge chair. He cleared his throat and then whispered, "I don't know, I wasn't really looking, but then I started noticing this particular girl.

I have my reservations about her sometimes, I think she is more trophy wife material than a real life partner with whom I can share things. For starters, she's much younger than I am; she is still not mature in her outlook on life. And then when I think about it, it all boils down to me just wanting to be loved."

Phoebe was silent at that, what a lucky girl. It also made her aware of how shallow she had been going about trying to assess men based on their material worth. Here, this rich guy was saying that he just wanted to be loved. His voice even cracked at that, like he genuinely meant it.

She felt embarrassed about her eager question now. Maybe, if she could see how he looked, then, she could adjust to being genuine, caring and besotted and upstage that girl he had in his affection.

He was seriously rich and he was sharing thoughts with her. That can only mean that he had some interest in her.

If only she could see his face. She almost groaned aloud.

"What type of man are you looking for Phoebe Bridge?" he asked interestedly.

Phoebe inhaled deeply before answering. After telling her about his immature girl, how would she frame her reply so that she could sound like a better option?

"You are assuming that I am single." she replied cheekily.

"That was an oversight," he said, a smile in his voice, "from what I can see of you in the half light you are very pretty so maybe it was a stupid assumption."

"No I am single," Phoebe said quickly. "I want to marry a man who can support me financially," she chose her words carefully, "and be kind to me and love me to distraction, and I want to marry someone in the Christian faith."

"Ah," he said contemplatively, "so tall dark and handsome does not figure on your list?"

"Well, these last couple of days I realized that tall dark and handsome cannot feed me when I am hungry," Phoebe said philosophically, "or fix the leaking roof over my parent's head, unless of course he is handy with tools."

He grunted, "practicality over sentiment. Very unusual in

a girl of your age."

"Ha," Phoebe snorted, "most women who rush into marriage never consider the practicality over the sentiment. People can't always live on love. Though I figure it helps when you are poor to like the person you are locked in poverty with."

Once more he threw back his head and laughed. "Phoebe... Phoebe...Phoebe. It is refreshing to hear your view on love. You have an honest view. Most women in my acquaintance will pretend that they love you, when all they love is the lifestyle. It's good when two people in a relationship can understand, from the get go, what they are in for."

He tapped his hands on the side of the chair. "If I were a rich suitor and said to you, 'Phoebe what do you desire the most right now?' What would you ask for?"

Phoebe giggled. "That's easy: a car would be a nice present. Nothing too expensive though, the neighbors would talk. But definitely a car."

He grunted, "and if I asked you to lunch, would you come?"

"But of course," Phoebe laughed, "you are rich aren't you? We could dine at the Villa Rose. I heard they have an exclusive restaurant overlooking the sea. I personally know the chef there; his name is Caleb Wright, my friend's husband. The food is to die for. You would pick me up from work in your high-end car; you would park in front of the building so that all the nosy girls in customer service could see me."

She sighed and continued dreamily, "you could greet me with a huge bouquet of roses—large velvety blood red petals. I have never gotten roses from a guy before."

She sighed, "I am getting too old for these fantasies, but they persist, unfortunately."

He said to her, "I don't think that would be hard for any

man to do for you Phoebe. I think it's all in the inspiration. When a man is serious about a woman, he becomes inspired to please her. Don't you agree?"

Phoebe bit her lip, she had never inspired a man before, except for that one guy who she dated for a week and then found out that he was mentally disturbed. Whichever girl had Abbas inspired would be one lucky girl.

"Uh oh," he said intruding on her thoughts, "I think I'm needed, there's Sonia heading this way. Take care of yourself Phoebe Bridge."

And just like that he left her alone once more and she realized that all the while they were talking the night sounds had faded away, now they came back with a bang and she heard Charles and his friends singing Toto's song, Africa.

All of a sudden she felt like dancing and wished that he had stayed; wished that she had gotten his number; wished that she had seen his face; wished that she could make out who he was in the crowd by the pool.

Chapter Seven

The party had ended at midnight and Phoebe hadn't spoken to Charles all night. She had found him at the back of the stage area, eating and laughing with his friends. She had deliberately avoided him when she saw him searching for her in the crowd and only chose to seek him out when she thought it was time to go home. She had not spoken to Ezekiel Hoppings either. Curiously, he always seemed to disappear when she spotted him in a group and headed toward him. Obviously, that lady Sonia Beaumont was wrong; Ezekiel Hoppings was not interested in her.

The party was a waste of time for her she had concluded when she was dropped home and the bus had driven off. She had spoken to that one guy in the dark and after that she had lounged around bored until she had made up her mind to seek out Ezekiel Hoppings.

Several men had asked her to dance, but they were big-bellied leeches with sweaty faces, she shuddered to think that they thought she would have said yes.

She quietly let herself into the house and headed to her room, at least the party had been a good escape from the scent of the neighborhood. She took off the red velvet dress and flung it onto the bed in disgust. When she had gotten into the bus the back had developed another tear along the seam. She wouldn't wear it again. Maybe her mother could use it to dust furniture.

She took the pins out of her hair and brushed it out. Her hair needed a serious trim, it was way longer than she liked to wear it; its wavy tentacles were flirting with her hips. She brushed it out slowly thinking about the conversation she had with that rich Arab guy. It was a pity she hadn't gotten to see his face. He had been really fun to talk to.

His voice had sounded as if he was handsome and she closed her eyes trying to picture him, it was such a pity he had gone off into the crowd, she hadn't seen anybody as tall and muscular as he was in the groups standing around.

She was such a klutz. If she hadn't decided to tone down her usual approach to men, she'd have gotten his number or something. She sat on the bed dejectedly. As far as she was concerned her life was back to square one.

She wanted to talk to somebody about it, but Erica was on her honeymoon and Tanya wouldn't appreciate being woken so late in the night. She usually got up at five in the morning to run with a group of women from church. They had never invited her to go with them and Phoebe thought of spitefully calling Tanya so that she could be groggy in the morning, but decided against it.

Her phone rang, just when she had made up her mind to call it a night and to rehash in her minds eye the extremely lovely place that Ezekiel called home.

"Hey," Charles said when Phoebe answered grumpily.

"Sorry about tonight," Charles said before Phoebe could chastise him for calling her so late.

"Nothing to be sorry about," Phoebe said almost feeling guilty that she had used him as her entrance to see what a rich person's party was all about. "I had an interesting time."

"Well, we were thinking," Charles cleared his throat, "not we...I was thinking, would you like to come to the beach with me tomorrow evening? My friends will be there...We usually carry food and listen to music and watch the sunset, or swim down to Duncan's Cove...there is a lovely white sand beach there."

"I don't think so," Phoebe said hesitantly. She wasn't guilty enough to go out with him.

"Their girlfriends usually come too," Charles said hurriedly, "all of them go to the Great Pond Church. We are good clean Christian young people—we aren't heathens you know." Charles was trying hard to keep the desperate wheedling out of his voice. He really liked Phoebe and the night had not gone as planned. He hadn't seen her even once through the whole evening.

"Okay," Phoebe said reluctantly, "I am not going on that bike though."

Charles chuckled, "Darren will pick us up in the bus."

"You guys are like a herd," Phoebe said snidely, "you all pack up and go out together, play music together, have fun together. It's sickening."

Charles laughed. "We all grew up in the same district and went to the same high school."

"How old are you?" Phoebe turned off her light and settled down in her bed, she had wanted to talk to somebody, why not Charles?

"Twenty-five," Charles said eagerly. "How old are you?"

"Twenty-four," Phoebe sighed. "It seems like just

yesterday I was eighteen. My mother constantly tells me that I'm turning into a dried up old maid."

"Twenty-four is young! You should loosen up a bit, have some fun."

"I'm not a fun person," Phoebe said morosely. "I really don't have any friends or hang out with anyone. I had friends in high school but I didn't want them to know where I live and because of that I really did not get to bond with anyone. I used to have one or two friends at church but there was a little incident with Chris Donahue and they have been treating me strangely ever since. These days I have to literally force them to include me on their committees and their ministries.

At least Erica used to hang with me but now she's married and Tanya, who is supposed to be my best friend at church, has her little girl group too. They even go exercising in the morning and share Bible texts and pray for each other. Nobody cares about me." She released a long pent up sigh.

"That's not true," Charles said eagerly lapping up Phoebe's confessions. She sounded genuinely sad, as if she had just gone to a funeral instead of a party. "Women are not sure if they should befriend you. Maybe they think that you will steal their men; and men are just in awe and afraid that you will rebuff them if they approach you."

Phoebe snorted. "Don't try to make me feel better. I have concluded that I'm just not a girl's girl or a guy's girl either. The men who are attracted to me are poor, ugly or mentally disturbed. I would have friends if I were rich; people treat me in a certain way because I am poor."

Charles gasped, "Phoebe that's not true."

"You don't know anything about it," Phoebe said tears seeping through her long eyelashes. She sniffed. "I am poor, that's why people treat me mean. If I just had money you'd see how fast everybody would be willing to please me."

Charles was silent for a while, he wasn't sure but it sounded as if Phoebe was crying, "Phoebe listen, I'm not rich and I have loads of friends. If people don't like the true you they are wasting your time. Money can only buy fair weather friends. As soon as you don't have any they will disappear."

Phoebe sniffed. "All rich women have a gaggle of friends that they air kiss and go to fabulous parties with."

Charles struggled not to laugh. "Phoebe you are watching too many movies. You know, when I used to work as a river guide at Mayfield Falls, we had all sorts of people visiting for vacation and one time this rich man looked at me enviously and said he wished he had my job because I was around nature all the time and living life simply. Sometimes it's the simple things that make a difference," he finished earnestly.

Phoebe wiped her face with the sheet and contemplated what he said. She was tired of constantly being Phoebe, always fretting about her poverty and lack of things. "Okay I'll come with you and your nerdy friends tomorrow. Tell them not to stare at me and make stupid remarks."

"Okay," Charles said gleefully. "It will be my pleasure to show you how to live simply."

*****

Phoebe went to work bleary-eyed the next day, she was feeling curiously depressed and down. Her bout of melancholy was exacerbated when her mother had asked her, in a voice heavy with fatigue, if she wanted porridge for breakfast. It was leftover from dinner and Phoebe had shaken her head sadly and headed out of the house weighed down with her home situation.

"What's the matter Miss Pretty?" Vanessa asked her while she was in the kitchen making hot cocoa.

Phoebe shrugged. Vanessa was the office gossip and the only person who persisted in befriending her. After initial overtures, people usually left Phoebe alone, another thing she attributed to her being poor. She had grown up pretty insular, in a one-room shack on her father's farm. Her life outside of her upbringing had been filled with pretense and she had a tendency to mistrust friendly overtures from people.

Friends usually wanted her to celebrate birthdays with them, go to restaurants with them or hang out at places where she needed to have money or wear the latest clothes. She had none of those and she didn't want anybody close enough to her to find that out.

Her natural reaction was to shut them out, insult them, and make them feel as bad as she felt most of the time.

Her psychoanalyzing from last night hadn't stopped, she realized.

"You can tell me," Vanessa said conspiratorially, "Is it Mr. King? Did he say something to you this morning?"

"No," Phoebe said putting a determined smile in her voice, "our supervisor is fine."

"Oh," Vanessa threw her hand up in the air, "so why are you so down?"

Phoebe felt like shocking her and she wanted the office grapevine to know that she had been rubbing shoulders with the rich and famous and Vanessa's method of spreading news was faster than anything else at the bank.

"Well, I went to Ezekiel Hoppings' mansion last night... was invited to a party."

Vanessa's eyes widened in shock. "The Ezekiel Hoppings."

Phoebe nodded, "I got back late so I have not really gotten back my bearings yet."

"How did you get invited to a party at Lion's Head?" Vanessa asked in awe. "My boyfriend, Craig, works at

Elevator Financials in Kingston and even his boss cannot get into the inner circle. And his boss is big."

Phoebe shrugged. "It's a long story, another time I will tell you." She left the kitchen and a shocked Vanessa, and then waited to be treated like a minor celebrity throughout the day.

She didn't have long to wait. Persons in the office were whispering when she passed by.

When it rolled around to lunchtime, she was looking forward to eating in the cafeteria and having the curious seek her out for conversation, but got the shock of her life when a Bentley drove up at the entrance to the bank.

A uniformed chauffer stepped out of the driver's seat with dozens of red velvet flowers and came into the bank. He found her around the customer service area preparing to go to lunch and handed her a card and the flowers.

"Miss Phoebe Bridge?"

Phoebe's eyes widened. "Yes..."

"Mr. er...Abbas would like the pleasure of your company for lunch."

"He does?" Phoebe asked in shocked.

The driver nodded and leaned in closer to her. "He wants to know if the Bentley was the right touch."

Phoebe giggled, "Oh it's fine."

The bank was unusually quiet, even the customers in the short line to the customer service area were staring at Phoebe and then at the car outside.

"Going to lunch," Phoebe said to no one in particular, leaving her flowers on the desk and almost floated to the front door of the bank.

Chapter Eight

When she slid into the back seat of the Bentley, she giggled uncontrollably. "I can't believe you actually know where I work..." her voice trailed off. "Ezekiel Hoppings?"

"In the flesh," Ezekiel said, looking at her seriously. "We had a nice chat last night and I woke up this morning determined to make some of your dreams come true."

"Oh, I am shocked," Phoebe said, looking at him.

He seemed different; he still had those ugly scars crisscrossing his face but they made him seem manlier, somehow. She couldn't put her fingers on exactly what it was.

Maybe it was the heady scent of the flowers she just sniffed or the euphoria of knowing that the people in her office was going to talk about her for days on end. "Last night you said your name was Abbas. At least now I know why you were avoiding me when I came seeking you out in the crowd by the pool."

"My name is Abbas," Ezekiel said steepling his fingers, "Ezekiel was my mother's choice Abbas my father's. Abbas means lion as I told you before, hence the name of my place here is Lion's Head."

Phoebe shook her head in awe. "Well, I am truly flummoxed."

"I presume your lunch time is an hour?" Ezekiel asked her suavely.

Why hadn't she noticed before that he had a smooth English accent, mixed with something else she could not pin point and that he smelled good?

"Oh yes, an hour," Phoebe parroted.

"Well, I understand that the Villa Rose's main chef Caleb Wright is on honeymoon, so I guess we will have to make do with his assistant."

Phoebe nodded again. "That's fine."

"So how is work going so far?" He asked her interestedly and Phoebe found herself cataloguing his features and trying to find some special feature on his face that she could enjoy looking at.

She hadn't stared at him directly before or taken him in properly. She had always felt an odd repulsion to imperfection and looking at him made her uncomfortable. She almost felt like gagging.

His nose was battered-looking and crooked. He had a scar from the end of his eyebrow to under his chin on the right side of his face and there were three on his forehead that gave him permanent looking frown lines. They puckered and clustered together and there was what looked like a burnt mark on his left jaw.

The complexion on his face was uneven, light areas mixed with dark splotches, like he had been burnt and he had bags under his eyes like he hadn't slept for weeks.

He was staring at her too and Phoebe wondered if he could see the rejection in her eyes.

He gently prodded her back to the present with a half-smile. "Work today so far?"

"Er...a bit boring. It's Monday, middle of the month routine stuff."

His teeth were yellow. She shuddered. How could she eat while looking at his teeth?

Surely he was rich enough to fix them and fix his scars?

His body was okay...more than okay. He was in a polo shirt and she could see his bulging biceps, not too big and not too small. He had a scar on his arm too but that she could live with. It started from his wrist and snaked all the way up his arm, in a thick line like a snake.

Banging body and a hideous face. His hair was thickly curly and he had it overly long, usually at church when she spotted him he had it short to his scalp. Now she realized that he had corkscrew curls with a spattering of gray at the sides.

"Phoebe?"

"Yes." Phoebe replied weakly.

"Are you okay with my scars? You are staring at me fixatedly, pretty much how I am staring at you, but I am sure for different reasons."

"What happened to you?" Phoebe asked, her eyes drawn once more to his face. The revulsion was not as immediate as it was before, but the thought of gagging was lurking at the back of her mind.

"When I was seventeen, my whole family: me, my twin brothers, both fifteen, my younger sisters, ten and eight and our parents were on our way from a family reunion in Al Ghabah. Father was piloting his personal Cessna. It developed mechanical problems, he crash-landed in a remote area and the plane was engulfed in flames. I was the only survivor, almost died in hospital but here I am."

"Your whole family died?" Phoebe asked aghast.

"Yes," Ezekiel shrugged. "I try not to dwell on it. Usually I don't give explanations for my scars but I find where you are concerned I am making several exceptions to the way I operate."

"You are?" Phoebe asked still unsure if what was happening was real.

"Yes Phoebe Bridge, I am."

They dined outside at Villa Rose on a deck that led all the way out to sea. For the first time in her life, Phoebe understood what first class treatment felt like from the moment they arrived.

Chris Donahue himself greeted them. He looked at Phoebe in shock but he quickly masked it. He then introduced Ezekiel to the host who was a pleasant faced gentleman who was eager to please.

She looked over at the blue Caribbean Sea and imagined that she didn't have work in the next twenty minutes and she was taking a leisure lunch with nothing else to do when she got home but to take a spa treatment.

"Where do you go when you zone out like that?" Ezekiel asked Phoebe curiously.

"In my mind building up fairytales. I wish I did not have to go back to work, that this could be my lifestyle." Phoebe said to him truthfully.

He had been in the process of sipping some water but he placed it back on the table.

"Is that so?"

Phoebe laughed self-consciously, "I am sorry. I am not usually so forthright with my thoughts. I don't know what's come over me."

"I like that about you." Ezekiel contemplated her seriously. His deep brown eyes were boring into hers as if he could see into her soul. Phoebe was the first one to uncomfortably look away.

"I hope you know that you can always be honest with me. I've been around long enough to be un-shockable."

Phoebe relaxed in her seat, she found Ezekiel both repulsive and strangely easy to be around. The sense of ease she felt when she spoke to him in the dark last night still persisted even though she could see his face.

She had to conclude that it was growing on her because she didn't feel to gag as she did earlier when she stared at him.

"So why did you choose Three Rivers church as your church?" she asked him interestedly.

"I was invited by Chris Donahue about three and a half years ago. He and I are practically neighbors up at Bluffs Head. He mentioned that he was a Christian and I mentioned that I was looking for a church community to spend some time with when I am in Jamaica. I happened to visit one day and the singing was excellent."

Phoebe nodded and then glanced at her watch and gasped. "Oh my, my time is up."

Ezekiel nodded. "Of course."

He snapped his fingers and the host came running. In no time they were on their way back to the bank.

"Maybe I should buy this bank so that I can extend your lunch hours," Ezekiel said contemplatively.

"You can do that?" Phoebe asked breathlessly.

Ezekiel laughed, "I can."

He didn't elaborate just smiled quietly and out of nowhere Phoebe felt a rush of attraction toward him. It wasn't only looks that made a person attractive, she was beginning to realize, it was also power. Suddenly Ezekiel Hoppings was not so bad looking.

He lifted her hand and kissed it. She felt a tingle race all the way to her toes and she gasped.

He closed his eyes briefly and then opened them a pleased gleam in them. "Thank you for having lunch with me Phoebe."

The smile she gave him when she left the car was puzzled. What on earth just happened in there?

She rubbed her hand in puzzlement as she headed into the bank. Her co-workers all stared at her, a new alertness in their eyes. Phoebe imagined that they were thinking that her life was suddenly interesting.

She picked up the flowers which she had left on her desk and inhaled its sweet scent. She went to the kitchen and put her flowers in a glass of water and found herself smiling in bemusement as the water overflowed the glass without her even realizing that the pipe was still running.

Chapter Nine

The rain was lightly drizzling when Phoebe left work, promptly at four. Charles and his friends were waiting for her outside and she briefly wondered if she was crazy—going to the beach with a bunch of people who were free at four in the evening.

She headed toward the bank's front door while Vanessa held it open for her.

"Phoebe, where are you going now?" she asked curiously.

Phoebe smiled. "To the beach with a group of friends."

"Wow," Vanessa looked at her enviously, "I had no idea you were so popular, first you go to lunch with someone in a Bentley and now you are off with friends. Usually you are reserved and keep a low profile."

Phoebe shrugged and headed into the bus. This time the boys made a concentrated effort to treat her normally. Their girlfriends were in the bus along with a girl Charles introduced as his sister.

Phoebe was squeezed up between her and another girl who was singing to the music loudly. They were already in their bathing suit tops and shorts.

Phoebe was sure that she was the same age as the girls but she felt so much older. They giggled about everything, but instead of freezing them out with one of her superior smiles, she made a concentrated effort to set her face in pleasant lines.

She smiled slightly. It was ironic that she had made that promise just last night and today she went out with the richest man in Jamaica, who seemed as if he liked her. A deep warm feeling enveloped her and she tried hard to temper the anticipation that was gripping her mind.

When they arrived at the beach, they headed to where the boys deemed their spot, which was under a palm tree. Everybody laid out their towels and threw their stuff on it. Phoebe had forgotten to bring a towel, so Charles patted a space beside him on his towel. It was broad enough and had the pattern of a lion on it.

Phoebe crouched down beside him gingerly and tried to avoid touching him. She felt slightly self-conscious in her one-piece bath suit, but the other girls were in much scantier apparel. They had run into the water as soon as they threw down their things and were squealing and laughing.

What did they find so funny? Phoebe tried to think 'simple' and lighten her mind, but she still found herself cynically wondering how they could be so happy when they didn't even have regular jobs?

Charles was looking out at the water, a smile lit up his face and he turned to her. "Want to get wet?"

"No." Phoebe frowned, "not yet."

"You don't mind if I run in do you?"

"No," Phoebe grinned, "run ahead. I'll just sit over here."

He ran toward the water in his red trunks and Phoebe spared a minute to admire his torso. He had a footballers body, lithe and not heavily muscled. She wondered if he played the game and then her mind wondered to his face. He was very good-looking and the Mohawk haircut that he wore fit his features perfectly. He was a nice enough fellow. She lay on her belly and watched as they frolicked in the water. Then his sister Pinky came out of the water and came to sit adjacent to her.

"I am so tired." She groaned glancing at Phoebe while she rummaged in her bag.

"Huh?" Phoebe looked at her properly for the first time. Charles had introduced them earlier but like the last time when he had introduced his guy friends, there were about five girls and she had been struggling to remember the names of each of them.

"Tired," Pinky said, dragging a chocolate bar from her bag. "Want piece?"

"No thanks," Phoebe said, "had a heavy lunch today."

"Ah," Pinky nodded, "with that rich guy."

"What? How'd you know that?" Phoebe asked looking at Pinky. She couldn't recall seeing her when she went to the villa, she would have remembered her. Pinky had her short natural hair dyed in a platinum blonde color. It should have clashed with her honey brown complexion but it didn't.

Pinky shrugged, "I work at Villa Rose, filling in for the receptionist. Don't know how long I'll be there though, Mr. Donahue, seems to dislike me."

"Is that so?" Phoebe asked looking at Pinky with new eyes.

"Well," Pinky said, "he finds fault with everything I do."

"Maybe because he likes you." Phoebe gave Pinky a knowing look. "You are a pretty girl."

Pinky giggled. "I doubt that. Mr. Donahue is obsessed with

some woman who designed the place. That's what I heard through the grapevine anyways."

"Her name is Kelly," Phoebe said sitting up, "and yes that obsession of his runs deep."

Pinky shrugged. "Enough about me. What are you doing with my brother if you are going out with that rich guy?"

"Hanging out," Phoebe said, surprised that she was so easy in Pinky's company.

"He likes you," Pinky said mournfully, "but I am sure you know that. And I am sure you will break his heart. My brother can't compete with the guy I saw you with at lunch."

"There is no competition going on. I'm just talking to the two of them."

Pinky sighed, raised her eyebrows at Phoebe and then silently chewed her chocolate bar.

Phoebe felt like defending herself but the opportunity was lost when Charles and his friends came back, talking and laughing.

"Where's the guitar?" one of the girls asked, "I want to hear music."

Darren ran to the bus and got it and the conversation ran to general subjects until he came back.

The guys all took turns playing and singing. Phoebe was actually enjoying herself with them. Somebody had brought cookies.

"Got it from the leftovers from the lunch buffet at my hotel," one girl said. She was short and fat and sitting on the lap of one of the guys. Phoebe had stopped trying to remember their names. Yesterday she had called him Sleazy, in her head.

Apparently there were quite a few leftovers because the girl had a whole container of cookies. They passed it around and chatted effortlessly, including Phoebe in their group as if she had always belonged.

When Charles got the guitar he cleared his throat. "Well this song is dedicated to my friend Phoebe."

Phoebe had been chewing her biscuit slowly; half listening to them, half thinking that they weren't such a bad group of people after all. She came to attention when Charles said that and looked at him sharply. "I hope it's not a love song."

"No," Charles replied when the laughing had stopped. He strummed the guitar and sang Bob Marley's song 'I'm Hurting Inside.'

He did such a good imitation of the singer's voice that tourists who were passing by stopped and listened. His voice wafted on the evening air as he strummed his guitar, the soulful song resonating with Phoebe.

She felt exactly like that, as if she was hurting inside. She desperately wanted to be happy. She had tears in her eyes when he finished playing and vaguely heard the clapping behind them. She closed her eyes and swallowed down the lump in her throat.

If only she could be at peace in her mind. If only she could accept life as simply as these young people did.

When she opened her eyes Charles was looking at her knowingly. He came and sat right beside her and then squeezed her fingers. She could smell his maleness and took a weird comfort in his presence.

Chapter Ten

Phoebe slept soundly that night. She had given in when everybody had encouraged her to take a dip in the sea and when she got home she had felt bone weary. Her mother had looked at her contemplatively and then went back to her reading with a small smile on her lips.

Phoebe was too tired to question her about the look but when she woke up in the morning her mother was sitting at the foot of her bed with a pleased smile on her face.

"Spill it," she said simply, staring at Phoebe. She had on a faded blue sari and looked like she had been up for hours.

"Spill what?" Phoebe asked glancing at her clock. It was five-thirty in the morning.

Nishta chuckled. "Can you imagine my absolute shock when one Mr. Ezekiel Hoppings called here last night while you were out? You left your cell phone on the center table in the hall, so naturally I answered it."

Phoebe groaned. "You spoke to him?"

"Of course," Nishta said smirking, "and then I called Willis to research the man on the Internet. Can you imagine what he found?"

Phoebe groaned again and pulled the sheet over her head. "I am not plotting anything with you. For once, can I please live my life like a normal woman?"

"He is the one," Nishta said, gleefully. "He is the man to get us out of this hell hole. He is the man for us...I mean you."

"He is not handsome," Phoebe mumbled under the sheet. "Remember you said that the two most important things in life are looks and money."

"When did I ever say that?" Nishta asked feigning shock. "Well if I did, I've changed my mind. The most important thing in life is money, at least for right now. And right now, money is pursuing you. If you mess this up Phoebe I don't know if I can forgive you."

Phoebe groaned. "Leave me alone."

Nishta got up off the bed. "Don't disappoint us Phoebe. That man is more than loaded and I don't like how you are suddenly going out with that boy from next door. You were at the beach with him...Have you lost your senses? Have you forgotten everything I have taught you?"

"I am trying to." Phoebe squinted up at her mother. "Last night I finally realized that I am like how I am because of you, and I hate it. I hate myself. Every time I try to be a better person your voice is in my head beating like a drum. Last night, for the first time in years, I felt happy, like how I could be if I were normal and didn't have you as a mother."

Nishta gasped. "You ungrateful wretch, I sacrificed my life to raise you." Tears came into her eyes. "All I want is the best for you. Why can't you understand that and why are you so ungrateful?"

Phoebe sighed and got up from the bed. "Stop pressuring me to pursue rich men and get married."

Nishta wiped away her tears and sniffed. "You deserve the best. Haven't I told you, time and time again, that with your looks you are entitled to the best in life?"

Phoebe sighed heavily and was about to retort when a knock sounded on the front door.

She looked at her mother curiously and then at the clock. When she peeped through her window, there was the same uniformed chauffer that had come to the bank yesterday and outside beside her rusty gate was a red Honda Civic with a big bow on it. She gasped. She had told him that night at the party that she would want a car as a gift. He was taking her seriously. The thought sent her sitting back on the bed hard. This was turning out to be her fairytale, except that she didn't love the man, and suddenly she felt guilty about the whole thing.

Nishta looked at her curiously and then almost tripped over her sari to look through the window.

When she saw the car she gasped. "Have mercy! There is a car with a bow out there."

She swerved around and looked at Phoebe a greedy gleam in her eyes. "I am loving this. Stop acting like this is a bad thing. Go and receive your present and look happy about it."

*****

Phoebe looked at the car keys in her hand and then at the car. Her mother had run outside as soon as the chauffer left and removed the bow. She sat in the car grinning like a Cheshire cat and honked the horn.

Her father had come outside to see what all the excitement was about and had looked at Phoebe and shook his head.

"You know Phoebe," his big brown eyes were sad, "your grandmother and namesake, God rest her soul, was a hardworking woman who bought the farm we now have with her own money. If her life hadn't been cut short, who knows what else she would've done under her own steam, you can do the same. I have told you time and time again that your mother is a bitter busybody who is chronically unhappy and living in the past. Don't let her make you into a gold-digger."

Phoebe had listened to him stony-faced. He had finally stopped his lecture after her mother had stood in the doorway and they were now bickering in the house. Only her mother's loud screeches could be heard and Phoebe walked even further down the walkway trying to drown her out.

She looked at the car again; it even had the plastic on the seats—it was brand new. In all her fantasizing about owning a car, she had forgotten that she couldn't drive.

A movement on the wall beside hers had her looking up swiftly. Charles was sitting on his wall out at his gate in a sleeveless shirt and a torn up jeans. He looked so handsome and fresh in the morning air. Phoebe who was otherwise impervious to good-looking poor men, found her heart melting a little when she saw him. Being attracted to Charles was coming at a very inopportune moment.

"Nice ride," Charles said looking over at the car.

"I...er...got it as a gift."

"Seems like the party paid off for you." Charles said casually.

Phoebe hugged herself. "I have no time to explain this."

"I know the basics," Charles said cynically. "You are pretty, he is rich. You are looking for rich, he is looking for pretty."

Phoebe looked at the car keys again and turned it over in her hand. "Stop sounding so jealous. I barely know you."

Charles shrugged. "You barely know him too and he's

giving you a car?"

"How do you even know who 'he' is?" Phoebe asked hotly.

"Pinky told me," Charles said. "You went to lunch with him yesterday and then hung out with me in the evening."

"It's not like that," Phoebe said defensively. "We go to the same church."

"And yet you had to crash his party." Charles scoffed.

"I didn't even know that it was his party...I don't have to justify myself to you." Phoebe stormed up the drive.

"I can teach you how to drive." Charles called out to her before she reached her veranda.

Phoebe spun around. "How did you know that I...never mind, do you have a license."

Charles nodded.

"Will this evening at four-thirty be alright?" Phoebe asked him huffily.

Charles nodded again. "I'll be here."

Phoebe waved him off and went inside the house.

Her parents had stopped bickering. Her father was lying in the settee looking unusually pensive and her mother was smiling and humming. They were both acting strange.

Phoebe left the house half an hour earlier than usual. Her world was turning upside down and she wasn't sure she liked it.

*****

At four-thirty every evening, for six weeks, she got driving lessons from Charles. Coincidentally, Ezekiel had to suddenly leave the country to divest his vineyard in Australia, he had gotten a serious offer for it and his presence was needed to negotiate the deal.

He called her every night though and they'd chat for long

periods of time. Initially Phoebe had felt awkward with Ezekiel and then she found that they had a lot in common. They both liked the same books and movies and even the same flavor ice cream.

He was so well spoken, mature and knowledgeable about so many things. It was a running joke between them that Phoebe would often have to go researching for the meaning of a term, in her battered encyclopedia, to find out what he meant, or he'd casually talk about a place and she had to go search her atlas to find out where on the globe it was. She had her encyclopedia and atlas beside her bed for easy access these days.

It seemed as if he had seen everything, been everywhere and in general had tasted all aspects of life. Phoebe wished she could have the privilege of doing some of those things too. He waxed lyrical about his Arab heritage and yet he made his home base Jamaica.

Phoebe realized that she was getting to like Ezekiel because of the time they spent together on the phone.

And yet, it was the opposite with Charles.

Charles was playful and took life easy. For him, if something were going to happen it would happen anyway, so why stress over it. He laughed a lot and loved music. He had started leaving CD's in her car radio. Sometimes he'd play a song for her and hum along. For Charles everything was music and fun and joy and lightness.

She looked forward to her driving lessons and her phone calls, but she found herself wishing that the two men could be a composite, and then she would have her perfect man.

*****

Erica had come back from her honeymoon and had

belatedly called Phoebe the day before to invite her to dinner.

"My first dinner party as Mrs. Wright. You are welcome to bring a guest. I heard that you are spending lots of time down at Great Pond church with a nice guy."

Phoebe had wanted to explain that Charles was not her guy but she couldn't deny that she had been spending all of her weekends down at his church or at their random gigs all over the town.

"Want to go to a dinner party with me?" Phoebe asked Charles when she got into the car later that evening. She could drive properly now and was getting to be a pro at parallel parking; she really did not need him to teach her anything else.

Charles grinned. "Are you asking me on a date?"

"Don't bother," Phoebe said huffily.

"You know you need to work on your temper," Charles said conversationally.

"You are exasperating," Phoebe rejoined swiftly.

"You are beautiful," Charles said grinning.

"Exasperating is not a compliment."

"I figured," Charles said crestfallen. "When is the dinner party?"

"Tomorrow at five. I made an appointment for my driving test next week Thursday. Do I have to study that little road code booklet thingy that they give you?"

"Yup," Charles said, "it should be a breeze for you to pass. You are bright—and if Howie can pass, I am sure you can too."

"Who is Howie again?" Phoebe asked genuinely puzzled.

"The one you call Sleazy, he's the one that is always staring at your breasts." Charles grinned as he drove the car slowly along the coastline highway toward Comma Point where they usually stopped to watch the sunset. The road was not usually very busy in the late afternoon, so Phoebe had found the place to be a great location to take her lessons.

Charles stopped at their regular place and looked over at her. She had her hair in one of those no-fuss ponytails she combed her hair in when she was going out with him—even without a lick of makeup she was gorgeous.

He wondered if she realized just how obsessed with her he had become. She treated him like a casual friend and he treated her the same, but only because he knew that Phoebe would drop him like a hot potato if he showed any untoward interest.

He felt like his time in Phoebe's life was temporary. She was like a beautiful butterfly you couldn't trap in a bottle without air and expect it to survive. He figured that was the way Phoebe felt about her life at Flatbush Scheme, as if she didn't have any air.

He wondered about her and Ezekiel Hoppings. Charles knew he wasn't around. He wondered if he and Phoebe spoke regularly.

He found himself wondering a lot about Phoebe and about what made her tick. His friends thought he was in over his head with her. His sister thought he was crazy to be teaching her to drive a car that was bought for her by another man. But he reasoned that he had to help her learn to drive. That he had enjoyed himself teaching her, he couldn't deny.

"Stop staring at me," Phoebe said elbowing him in the side.

"Just thinking," Charles said staring ahead, "want to hear some music?"

Phoebe nodded, and he pushed the CD in the player and deliberately played Dennis Brown's version of the song, 'Any Day Now.'

"The lyrics are so sad," Phoebe said looking at him.

Charles shrugged, "I feel like that about you: any day now,

you'll be gone."

"That's not fair," Phoebe protested, "we are just friends and we live beside each other. With my luck, I'm not going anywhere anytime soon."

Charles watched her pink lips as she spoke and turned into his seat, watching her intently. He moved closer to her, they were almost nose tip to nose tip. Phoebe inhaled noisily.

"Don't," she protested weakly.

"Why not?" Charles asked, "because I am poor?"

Phoebe closed her eyes and he touched his lips to hers.

The first contact was like electricity running between the two of them. He kissed her deeply, her lips tasted like peppermint and chocolate.

Phoebe clutched his shirtfront while the kiss deepened; his lips were soft and where their lips connected her nerve endings were jumping.

The kiss was neither demanding nor gentle.

It was perfect.

Her first real kiss.

They pulled away in mutual agreement and they both stared ahead. Phoebe felt muddled and mixed up inside. Like she had gone too near fire and was singed.

Chapter Eleven

Erica's dinner party coincided with a wet afternoon and when Phoebe got into the car with Charles she was feeling as gloomy as the evening. Last night when she had gotten home she had spoken to Ezekiel as usual, but her mind had been on the kiss.

"What's wrong?" Ezekiel had asked, a note of awareness in his voice indicated that he knew she wasn't totally into the conversation with him.

"Nothing," Phoebe had responded, still thinking about that kiss with Charles.

He had spoken to her some more but she had hardly heard. He had hung up the phone after a few minutes sounding pensive. It was the shortest time they had ever spoken together over the phone since he was in Australia. Phoebe felt a pang when she glanced at the time, but she couldn't stop herself from touching her lips and staring up into her stained ceiling, reliving the experience.

She felt torn inside, and seeing Charles in the flesh today made her feel even more torn.

Why did she even invite him to Erica's? Was she going nuts?

Charles was poor, and she was now closer to her goal of marrying rich. Ezekiel had declared his intention to woo her. Men didn't just up and buy cars for anybody; neither did they spend hours on the phone with a woman just so they could get to know her. She realized that Ezekiel was serious and yet here she was, dithering about a guy who lived beside her in Flatbush Scheme.

She wasn't acting herself; the temptation to give back Ezekiel his car and to live a simple life with Charles was actually in her thoughts last night.

Charles greeted her in his effusive manner when he got into the car and Phoebe looked at him with a small smile on her face. Charles was effortlessly handsome; he had on a green t-shirt with the name of his band scrawled across the front and well-fitting blue jeans.

"I hope I'm not under-dressed?" He gave her long orange dress a once over. "You look gorgeous. If you had on a pair of green eyes you'd look just like a curly-haired Aishwarya Rai."

"Thanks," Phoebe murmured, "my mother always says that. About the kiss..."

Charles held up his hand. "No post mortem over the kiss, I know you are about to give me a speech and I don't think I want to hear it."

Phoebe smiled. "Okay then."

When they arrived at Erica's, Phoebe was still struggling in her mind about the kiss, about Ezekiel and about her shifting views.

Erica and Caleb were staying at Kelly's place until their

house in the hills was refurbished. It was the first time Phoebe was actually going inside and she found it spacious and really elegant.

The kitchen was obviously the hub of the house; half of it was in glass, giving the inside an outdoorsy feel. You didn't have to crane your neck to see the sea in the distance while sitting at the breakfast nook; Phoebe liked that feature very much.

Caleb was at the stove, stir-frying something.

"It smells lovely in here." Phoebe grinned at Caleb while she and Charles sat at the nook watching.

Erica was flitting around the kitchen looking for some special glasses. They chitchatted about the places they had been to in Paris and the things they had seen on their honeymoon.

As soon as it was politely possible, Phoebe dragged Erica from the kitchen, leaving Charles with Caleb who had started talking about sports. They stood in what looked like the living room it had hardwood floors and a dome-shaped ceiling.

"What's wrong?" Erica asked her concerned.

"I am in trouble." Phoebe looked at Erica panicked.

Erica sat in an armchair her feet hanging over the side and raised her eyebrow. "I thought you were saving your virginity for the highest bidder."

"You guys got married just eight weeks ago and already you are raising your eyebrows like Caleb?" Phoebe asked exasperated.

Erica giggled, "I didn't even realize I was doing it. What's wrong Pheebs? You look positively shaken. Are you really in 'pregnant trouble'?"

"No," Phoebe said fanning her off, "it's worse than that. I like Charles," Phoebe whispered fiercely. "I really, really like him—like flowers and lollipops and rainbows in the sky kind of like."

"Aww," Erica grinned, "what a relief to hear that you are not preggo and that you like a guy. Is the air fresher, the grass greener? Do flowers sing when you walk by?"

"I knew you wouldn't take this seriously," Phoebe said fiercely. "Don't you see that Charles is all bad for me? For one, he is poor; he works as an entertainment coordinator at a hotel. Two, he has no ambition. Last week he told me that he is content to be an entertainment coordinator as long as the hotel wants him to be. Three, he thinks Scrabble is a game involving eggs. Four, his one great goal for the foreseeable future is to buy a bigger bike next year."

"But he has a car, a nice one too," Erica said. "Isn't that one of your criteria for choosing a man? And he's also handsome don't forget that."

Phoebe groaned and sunk down in a chair across from Erica, "I got the car as a present from Ezekiel Hoppings. Problem is, Ezekiel likes me, like really likes me, and I talk to him every night on the phone."

Erica gasped. "Wowser! How'd you get yourself so busy? I was only absent for two months enjoying my fabulous honeymoon." She grinned wickedly. "Caleb can do things with his tongue a sanctified ear should not hear! When we got home from the wedding we almost did it on the steps outside."

"Enough already," Phoebe grimaced, "don't say a word more, and stop licking your lips like that."

Erica laughed out loud. "Okay, okay, tell me what's been going on with you and your men, from the beginning, and hurry. Caleb is just putting some finishing touches on the meal."

Phoebe spoke as fast as she could.

Erica listened attentively and then tapped her chin thoughtfully, "I think this is your test. This is the moment in your life when you have to let go of your prejudices about looks and poverty and everything else you have stored up in that busy mind of yours. I personally think you should give back the car and let Ezekiel down gently and then see where it goes with Charles. But then again, I realize that you are the one who has to make the decision."

Phoebe stood. "But Erica, this is it. This is my opportunity to release myself from poverty and to be truly happy."

Erica dragged herself out of the sofa too and put her hand on Phoebe's shoulder. "You need to stop seeking happiness for itself and seek God. He's the only source of happiness. I can assure you that riches will not make you happy. You are still young and you have some horrible views on life, men, and money. I have no idea where those views came from, but from personal experience, I can tell you that money can't buy you happiness. It can buy you loads of stuff but it can't fill that unhappiness hole."

Phoebe thought about what Erica said and grumbled, "It's easy for you to be spouting these little gems at me but you never grew up like I did, did you? You have never lived in Flatbush Scheme, or worked at a job for peanuts. Erica, I have no trust fund or doting Daddy with supermarkets all over the North Coast."

Erica squeezed her hand. "I have faith that you will come to your senses about this whole happiness and riches thing when you sit down and really think about it. Anyway, let's go join the fellas and see if they missed us."

When they returned to the kitchen Caleb and Charles were having a lively discussion about football and hadn't missed them one bit.

All throughout dinner, Phoebe looked at Charles as he

interacted with Erica and Caleb. He was funny and relaxed and she could see why he was such a natural at his job, but was he the right person for her?

She squelched her sigh while staring at the food in her plate.

*****

Phoebe spent the following week reading her driver's test booklet and trying to memorize the signs and signals. Charles would give her a quiz when he got home from work and would laugh at her if she didn't get the basics right.

She had not heard from Ezekiel since the evening she kissed Charles. It was as if he had sensed that her distraction was because of another man.

She missed his calls though; she missed his dry sense of humor and his recounting of some of his adventures in diverse parts of the world that he usually painted vividly for her.

She couldn't explain the conflict that was going on in her mind and she valiantly tried to ignore her burgeoning attraction to Charles and the war tugging at her mind about Ezekiel.

She did her driver's test on Thursday and passed it. Charles took her to Vanley's Veggie Pub to celebrate. It was a grass shack by the beach that served vegetable juice in shot glasses and big tumblers of weirdly named vegetable concoctions.

Vanley was a cancer survivor who was miraculously healed by carrot juice. He never got tired of telling his story. He was in the middle of recounting his story when they walked in. He waved to Charles and whistled at Phoebe.

Phoebe was shocked at how many people were in the circular shack which had a straw roof and a round bar table.

People were chugging down vegetable and fruit juices and snacking on strange looking snacks. There was a small chalkboard on the front of the shack that advertised the brew for the day. She had to double check if she was seeing right when she saw the words Seaweed Juice.

"Ew," she turned to Charles. He had on a blue Oxford shirt and black dress pants. She had never seen him so dressed up before and when he had accompanied her to the driving depot she could not keep her eyes off him. As soon as they left the depot, though, he had undone all the buttons and dragged his shirt out of his pants.

"I hate the formal thing," he had looked at her apologetically.

Phoebe had shrugged because even in his scruffy state he was handsome.

"Welcome Empress," Vanley said loudly, almost bowing to his knees when he saw Phoebe. "Charlie, is your chick this? She looks like she drinks vegetable juice all day. Beautiful." He smacked his lips obscenely.

Phoebe laughed and Charles gave him a high-five.

They sat down on a bar stool and Charles ordered the usual.

"How do you know about this place?" Phoebe asked Charles curiously.

Charles laughed. "We play here sometimes. Vanley pays us with drinks and his delicious seaweed chips."

Phoebe shuddered again. "Seaweed chips? I never pegged you as a raw food lover."

Charles smiled. "Vanley's story about his survival from cancer can move even the most avid skeptic to rethink the concept of eating for health. Once more the concept of 'simple' is working here. Rich foods with elaborate ingredients may not be the best for your digestive system. A poor simple plant may be the best thing for you even though it is growing next door in Flatbush Scheme rather than in an exotic bush in Bluffs Head."

Phoebe smiled, "I hear your analogy, duly noted."

Vanley placed before them two large pineapples husked out and filled with juice. The juice tasted like pineapple mixed with papaya and acerola cherries.

Phoebe sipped through the straw and hummed, "this is good."

Charles smiled, his brown eyes lighting up with glee. "Told you: 'simple' is better."

*****

Phoebe was happily sipping and grinning with Charles when Ezekiel walked in. He had to bend his head to prevent the straws that were hanging around the shack from grazing his head. He looked around in the semi dark interior and his eyes zeroed in on Phoebe. She was laughing at something the guy she was with said.

She threw back her head and laughed in wild abandon. He had never seen Phoebe like that before—so relaxed and free.

The guy, Charles Black, wiped a speck of juice from her chin. It was a revealingly intimate gesture. She looked at Charles, a smitten look on her face.

Ezekiel's heart clenched in fear. He had heard her tone of voice the last they spoke and had rapidly closed the negotiations in Australia to return to Jamaica.

He had bided his time while his security detail gave him a full report on Phoebe's whereabouts for the time he was off the island, and what he read scared him.

He had found out belatedly that she couldn't drive. He acknowledged painfully that he had practically set her up with Charles Black. According to the security reports, they had been inseparable for the past few weeks.

He felt like hitting his head on something hard.

How could he compete with Charles Black? He was younger, handsome, not tied down by any responsibility and he lived beside Phoebe. She had obviously forgotten her conviction about marrying for practicality rather than sentimentality, if the doe eyes she was making with Charles was any indication.

He left the restaurant and sat in the back of the Bentley. Should he leave the situation as it was? There were so many options running through his head. He could always use his money to woo back Phoebe. She obviously has a soft spot for him. She had kept the car that he gave her, hadn't she?

But did he want her on those terms?

Did he want a woman who only wanted him for his money?

He contemplated that on his way to Lion's Head and he contemplated it over dinner, which was a lonely affair. He had planned to invite Phoebe up to the house tonight but the security detail he had trailing her had told him she was at Vanley's Veggie Bar with Charles Black.

He contemplated it until he couldn't sleep. He went walking alone by the seaside, hoping that the sound of the sea would soothe his active mind.

Why didn't he just dismiss Phoebe as another gold digging woman after his fortune? God knows, he had encountered several of them in his lifetime. And he had found that trait, even in the most beautiful of women, as ugly as the scars on his face.

But then he remembered the conversations that he had with Phoebe on the phone, he pictured her pretty face upturned to his and smiling. He wanted her; he wanted to have her around him everyday. He needed those lips to smile for him exclusively. He wanted her in his bed every night. He wanted to explore her both inside and out and he didn't care if she was a gold-digger.

He gritted his teeth and sat down in the sand. If he married her, how could he keep her? How would he live with himself knowing she was unhappy with him, knowing that she yearned for that boy Charles Black.

The thought was enough to have him gritting his teeth.

In the wee hours of the morning he made up his mind that he would try for Phoebe one more time.

One more time he would extend himself. He would allow himself to be rejected by her. If she pushed him away he would leave it there. It would be hard, his whole essence was taken up with Phoebe but the years would loosen this intense feeling he had for her.

If she didn't push him away he would marry her, she could grow to love him as he would love her.

The ball would be put squarely in Phoebe's court. He would allow her to decide.

Chapter Twelve

Phoebe's cell phone rang early Friday morning; she looked on the screen and saw Ezekiel's number—she was tempted not to answer and to turn it off. She almost did it too, but she remembered the car outside and her finger reluctantly pressed the talk button; she stared at it as if it was not a part of her body.

"Hey Ezekiel."

"Good morning Phoebe." Ezekiel sounded crisp and business like.

"Morning." Phoebe sat up in the bed, feeling slightly tense; he sounded brusque like he meant business.

Ezekiel paused. "I've been invited to a party in Cayman this weekend. Want to come?"

"Cayman?" Phoebe gasped, "as in outside of Jamaica?"

"Yes," Ezekiel replied cagily. He sounded reserved, quite unlike the relaxed man she had been talking to the past few weeks.

Phoebe's mind raced, she had all but made up her mind to give him back the car. If she went to Cayman with him, what would that make her—the gold digging opportunist that her mother had carefully reared for years?

She liked Charles. He was fun and simple, and for the first time in years she didn't care that a man had no prospects or money in the bank. She would not call what she felt for Charles love; maybe it was a crush. The feeling was strange to her, but she actually felt willing to explore it some more.

She looked around her in the gloomy room and inhaled. If Ezekiel but knew what he was asking her to choose with this trip. This was the pivotal point. She was supposed to go to a church social with Charles and his lively group of friends on Saturday night and then they were playing at an event in Fairview on Sunday night. Charles said he was going to play a song just for her.

She sighed. Seconds were ticking by. Ezekiel was quiet over the phone. It was as if he was hardly breathing. He didn't say a word to convince her one way or the other, no coercion, nothing.

She clutched her cell phone tighter.

Money or Love?

Money or Love?

Phoebe inhaled deeply. "Do I need a visa to go to Cayman?"

Ezekiel exhaled loudly. "I will work out the details by the end of the day. Pack lightly. I ordered clothes to be delivered to the house for you."

"Huh?" Phoebe asked surprised. He was that sure of her response.

"In anticipation of your coming with me I gave a personal shopper your size and she got you some things. The clothes will be there before we land in Cayman this evening."

Phoebe's heart leapt with anticipation, these were the kind

of things that having money could do for you. "Wow."

"I'll send George to pick you up from work at four-thirty. I'll see you at my private airstrip."

Phoebe gulped again. "Private air strip?"

"Yes," Ezekiel said, a smile in his voice, "I travel too often to use regular air transportation. I'm really looking forward to this weekend Phoebe." His voice softened. "Thank you for accepting."

Phoebe got up from the bed reluctantly when Ezekiel hung up. The conversation with Charles would not be easy. She was tempted to just tell him, face-to-face, that she wasn't going to be around, but she didn't want to see his expression or his disappointment in her. She'd call him during her lunchtime and tell him that she wasn't going to be around this weekend.

Her mother was sitting in the hall crocheting when Phoebe entered the cramped space—her fingers happily flying over the thread. She was also humming her favorite song, 'Yeh Kahaan Aa Gaye Ham,' a Hindi romantic song, which always made her excited.

Her mother had always sung it to her to put her to sleep when she was young. It was based on a movie called Silsila. A movie about star-crossed lovers who finally ended up with their true loves in the end, after much drama.

Her mother used to tell her the story in both Hindi and English. She wondered about the irony of her mother humming that song at this time of the morning and looking so happy.

Phoebe had to pause to look at her. She could pinpoint the last time she had seen Nishta smile and look contented, it was the time she had convinced Phoebe to enter that beauty pageant. She had been filled with such joy, in anticipation of Phoebe winning, that she had been smiling all day, up until

Phoebe had placed third. Her smile had vanished for years and was just now re-emerging.

"Why are you so happy?" Phoebe asked grumpily.

"Because my daughter is sorting out her life properly," Nishta said happily. "Just the way I taught her. A mother has to be happy for that."

Phoebe grunted, "I am going to Cayman with Ezekiel this weekend."

"You are?" Nishta squealed, "How fabulous! This is serious business Phoebe. Don't mess it up."

Phoebe groaned. "I don't know if I should keep on encouraging him? I am of two minds. I like Charles. He's so easy to be around."

Nishta knit her brows and hauled herself from the sofa, throwing down her thread. "Look at me Phoebe," she said a heartrending fierceness in her eyes. "If you give up this opportunity, you are looking at yourself in twenty-four years. Do you hear me?"

Phoebe scowled, "I will not let myself get fat like you, and Charles does have a job. He's an entertainment coordinator at a large hotel."

Nishta laughed. "I hated fatness too and Larry did have a job. I thought that love could conquer all. I defied my parents, said goodbye to my heritage, and look at me now. Look Phoebe," Nishta sneered, "don't you think I was pretty too? Don't you think I had flawless skin and a tiny waist? Don't you think I saw possibilities in our one-acre farm? Don't you think I thought that our one room hut was quaint but livable? Don't you think," tears sprang to her mother's eyes, "that I wanted to go back to school. I had dreams, big dreams."

Nishta pointed at Phoebe. "I had ambition. I wanted to grow. I wanted to have it all, but the thing is Phoebe, my looks faded overtime, hastened by poverty and worry. You won't have those looks forever my dear girl. Remember that."

She passed Phoebe and went into the kitchen. "Since your father has finally gotten off his haunches and gotten a job, I have eggs for breakfast. Want some?"

Phoebe stood in the hall, digesting all that her mother said, and empathizing with her. "No, I'm in the mood for something more exotic like smoked salmon or a quiche."

Her mother grinned. "That's the spirit girl. That's the Phoebe I grew and love. Never you ever dare settle for less than good enough."

She went back to humming her Hindi song and Phoebe sat down in the settee feeling unsure and unhappy once more.

What if settling with Charles wasn't really settling?

What if love was better than money?

*****

They arrived in Cayman, some minutes after five. Ezekiel had spent almost all his time on the phone in his onboard conference room. However, his personal assistant, Nathan, checked in on her every five minutes to ensure that she was comfortable.

"Boss' orders," he said, grinning. He was a tall, thin, white guy with a bookish air; he looked to be in his early thirties. "Mr. Hoppings is once more offloading one of his company's in Brazil. He is just putting things in motions, so he'll not be taking long."

He came and sat across from Phoebe. "I'm his right hand man you know. I've been working with him for seven years now."

Phoebe nodded, feeling overwhelmed. She had had no

idea how the inside of a jet looked. She was surprised to see that the images of planes she had in her head, with rows and rows of seats, was somewhat different from the one she now found herself in. It had seats facing each other, as well as a bedroom suite and a conference room.

The pilot had saluted her and the airhostess had given her a gift basket of fruits when she sat down. She had also itemized a long list of things that Phoebe could have for her comfort and enjoyment, just by asking.

Ezekiel had kissed her on the cheek and left her to her own devices.

She looked at Nathan who was skipping through a business magazine and trying to chat with her. She didn't expect him to entertain her, but she understood that when the boss ordered something it had to be done.

Nathan had been valiantly trying to chat with her without probing or revealing anything about his boss. It was a struggle for him because each time he looked at her, she could see curiosity beaming through his intelligent gaze.

"So where do you live Nathan?" She asked him.

"Anywhere Mr. Hoppings lives," Nathan said happily. "My job has no starting or ending hours and the staffing quarters on all his properties are more luxurious than any hotel."

"Sounds hectic," Phoebe said sympathetically.

"No, not for me," Nathan said, "I am single. My boss travels to exotic locales at the drop of a hat. I love it. When I applied for the post I had just graduated from law school. I had no idea it was so hard to get a decent job if you are not from one of those brand name law schools." He shook his head. "I applied for this job and got it. I will never practice law now."

"Right." Phoebe nodded.

Ezekiel came into the main cabin and Nathan got up. He

was in a charcoal gray business suit and his hair was neatly trimmed. He looked powerful and vibrant and he moved with an elegance that belied his size.

"Sorry about that Phoebe," he said, "I have this farm in Brazil that is getting some serious offers from two very determined bidders."

"No problem," Phoebe nodded, "how big is it?"

Ezekiel sighed, "It's a modest holding, just five hundred acres. I farm cattle there."

Phoebe tried valiantly not to let her jaw drop. Five hundred acres was modest? How rich was he?

She contemplated this in her head for a while and then they were reminded to put on their seat belts. They had arrived on a private landing strip near what looked like a sprawling resort.

"Wow," Phoebe said when she alighted from the jet. "What hotel is this?"

"Welcome to Lion's Gate," Ezekiel said grinning down at her, "my private residence in Cayman."

Chapter Thirteen

The mansion had a beach for the front yard and was made of cut stone and glass—she could barely take in all the features of the place. When Phoebe remembered to close her mouth, she was standing in a living room with two spiral staircases leading to doors on a balcony surrounded by delicate wrought iron balustrades. There were four mature palm trees in the middle of the living room, which had several towering glass windows through which one could gaze at the sea view.

Ezekiel was looking at her closely. "I trust you like the place?

"It's awesome," Phoebe whispered looking at him and smiling. "It looks even more spectacular than Lion's Head."

Ezekiel chuckled, a shaft of sunlight caught his eyes and Phoebe realized that his eyes were chocolate brown and his lashes were thick and curly. She hadn't realized that before and she also hadn't realized how ugly his scars were today.

In the grand scheme of things, she reasoned prosaically,

his scars were a minor issue. They were beginning to matter less and less to her.

He caught her looking at him with a look of puzzlement in her eyes and he gave her a lopsided smile. "Let me show you to your room."

Phoebe followed him up the spiral staircase and into a room with floor to ceiling glass, which opened onto a private balcony. She could hear the sea so clearly from the room that she knew she was going to have a good night's rest.

After showing her around and teaching her how to operate the gadgets needed for her comfort, Ezekiel looked at her. "I hope you don't mind me alone for company this weekend. I rarely keep staff here. Nathan usually heads to the staff quarters. We won't see him until we head back on Sunday night."

Phoebe inhaled nervously. "We are not sharing the room are we?"

Ezekiel raised one eyebrow. "Would you want to?"

"No," Phoebe stammered.

Ezekiel approached her and stood directly in front of her, towering over her and almost touching her. "I would want to. I think about us together pretty much everyday."

Phoebe's heart leapt a mile a minute.

He bent his head and kissed her gently on her lips. He nibbled a bit on her lips and then kissed her deeply.

It was electrifying, Phoebe closed her eyes and her lips clung to his. When he raised his head Phoebe was trembling.

He was staring at her in an intent way. "I want us to get to know each other in person. We already did the phone thing. This kiss proves we have chemistry. Not a bad move for a man who is intent on getting the most beautiful girl in the world to love him."

Phoebe gasped.

He touched her cheek gently. "I'll be cooking dinner. You can come and join me in the kitchen downstairs."

Phoebe sat on the bed shell-shocked when he left the room.

Chemistry, between her and Ezekiel Hoppings? A few weeks ago the thought would have been laughable, but these days her world was really topsy-turvy and she had strayed from her exacting preferences in men.

She liked and kissed a handsome guy, who was poor, and just now she kissed an ugly guy who was rich, she threw herself across the bed and admitted that both of them were great kissers.

*****

Phoebe had opened up the closet after she had stirred herself from her feverish thoughts of Charles and Ezekiel and found it full of obviously expensive clothes that were all in her size—she loved them all. She had only ever seen this kind of quality clothes in those snooty shops where the sales person followed her around because she wasn't known.

After a shower she put on a long hot-looking pink maxi dress and a soft slipper of the same shade. She chose to let down her long black hair and put on some pink lip-gloss, she assessed herself in the mirror. She looked and felt like a princess; the setting really complimented her.

"Watch out world." She whispered to her reflection.

She found Ezekiel in the kitchen making something that smelled really good. He looked up when she entered, a tender look in his eyes. "You look spectacular."

"Thank you." Phoebe smiled back at him.

"I am making smoked sausage jambalaya."

"Hmm, that sounds good. I had no idea you could cook."

Ezekiel chopped up the onions and garlic efficiently, and

threw them in the pot.

"My mother made sure that I could. She was adamant that all her boys would grow up doing the practical things. When my father protested that she was teaching me to do girl's things she would laugh."

Phoebe leaned her head to the side and viewed him coquettishly. "I thought that rich people weren't bothered by these menial things and have maids and butlers and gardeners and all manner of service people."

Ezekiel laughed. "Service people are necessary only because I'm too busy doing other things, but I like being alone sometimes. I do have staff here but usually when I am coming I have the place stocked for my comfort and stay here alone. These past ten years, I hardly come by this particular house, I'm afraid my business associates and friends stay here more than I do. I just had it re-decorated the other day, it was languishing in neglect."

They had dinner by candlelight in the kitchen alcove as they listened to the waves on the seashore.

He looked dark and mysterious in the half-light and Phoebe's new awareness of him was causing her pulse to beat erratically.

What on earth was happening to her? She tried to drum up her feeling of repulsion toward him but she kept remembering how drawn she had been to him from the earlier days of seeing him at church, even though she had always thought him ugly. Now suddenly her opinion of him was undergoing a metamorphosis because of that kiss. Or was it because she realized how rich he was. Was the lure of money that powerful?

He kept her laughing through dinner with tales of his trips to various countries and Phoebe found him to be entertaining. The food was also extremely good.

"Have you had many girlfriends?" Phoebe asked suddenly. She had been itching to ask. Was he planning to make her another notch on one of his expensive beds?

Ezekiel scratched his chin. "Let's see, a woman would ask a man that question because a, she wants to be a girlfriend, or b, she kissed him and found out that there was passion between them, or c, she's jealous."

Phoebe could feel her cheek growing warm. "Forget I asked."

"Not many girlfriends," Ezekiel said, his eyes twinkling. "Believe it or not this whole tycoon business does not leave space for much romance. I will have to seriously cut back on my traveling and interests in the near future. I want a wife, I want children and I want a home life."

Phoebe's heart pumped erratically. "That lady, Sonia, that told me off at the poolside is up for the role, isn't she?"

Ezekiel laughed softly. "No. My interest is in one Phoebe Bridge. She knows I want her. She just wants me to say it out loud."

Phoebe hung her head and worried her bottom lip with her teeth.

"The question is," Ezekiel pushed her hair away from her cheek, "how do you feel about me?"

Phoebe looked at him and then out the window into the darkness. "I am not sure."

"That's good enough for me," Ezekiel said briskly. "Let's get married tomorrow."

Phoebe looked at him and gasped. "You are not serious."

Ezekiel grinned, "I would be, if you were sure of your feelings. I would be honored to love and cherish you forever. But of course, I know you have to sort out your feelings toward Charles Black and I know my kind of lifestyle will take a lot of getting used to."

Phoebe's mind was racing, no it wouldn't, she had always wanted this lifestyle and how did he know about Charles?

"There is nothing to sort out with Charles," she said lightly, "and I thought marriage was a big deal especially for rich men? And shouldn't we go for counseling to find out if we are compatible."

"I know we are compatible," Ezekiel said, "that kiss and your response proved it. I would prefer spending time with you to find out if we are compatible than with a counselor."

Phoebe looked at him contemplatively. "Then that's what we'll do then, spend time together."

Ezekiel took up her fingers from the table and kissed them one by one. It caused a tingle to run through her body and when he released her fingers Phoebe put them in the other to stop them from trembling.

Chapter Fourteen

Phoebe and Ezekiel went to church together for the first time; Phoebe wore a powder blue dress and a matching hat. She loved the ensemble and on her way to church was wondering if she could keep all the gorgeous clothes that were in the closet at the house. She felt curiously euphoric and had slept peacefully last night, after Ezekiel had walked her to her door. She woke up this morning feeling as if she was on the verge of some major discovery.

When they drove up to the building, it looked plain enough on the outside but when she entered the church she could see, through the widows, that there was a lake and a garden to the side of the building. It would make a picturesque spot for a wedding and Phoebe allowed her mind to wander on about weddings.

Last night Ezekiel had insinuated that he wanted to marry her as soon as possible and she castigated herself for not accepting and going forward with it. This morning she would have been Mrs. Ezekiel Hoppings, with all the wealth and privileges that the title came with.

She would finally be where she was supposed to be in this life. Why she had held back is anybody's guess. Ezekiel was still ugly and that wasn't going to change, she thought about Charles, he was all the way back in Jamaica and he was not going anywhere anytime soon.

"Phoebe Bridge," a bright voice said behind her. When Phoebe turned around it was Kelly Palmer. She had her toddler in her lap and he was trying to reach for Phoebe's hair.

"Hi Sister Kelly," Phoebe smiled, "how are you?"

Kelly smiled. "I am fine and quite pleased to see you." She then looked at the man beside Phoebe and gasped, "Ezekiel Hoppings?"

Ezekiel turned around and gave her a smile. "Nice to see you again Kelly."

Phoebe looked at the little boy in Kelly's lap—he was the spitting image of Chris Donahue. Now she realized why they didn't carry him back to Jamaica for Erica's wedding. He didn't have any of Kelly's features. She wondered how they were dealing with the situation—Kelly appeared happy and relaxed to her.

"Where's Pastor Theo?" Phoebe asked curiously unable to drag her eyes from the toddler.

"He's outside," Kelly said, a note of discomfort in her voice at the way that Phoebe was staring fixedly at her son.

Phoebe finally dragged her eyes away from him and asked, "what's his name again?"

Kelly was looking like she regretted calling to Phoebe now. "His name is Mark."

"He looks just like Chris," Phoebe whispered in fascination. When she saw the mutinous look in Kelly's eyes she realized that she had spoken out loud.

Ezekiel stiffened beside her. He had been listening to their conversation but had faced forward; he turned around just then and smiled apologetically at Kelly.

Kelly shrugged. "It is what it is." She looked at both Ezekiel and Phoebe and raised her eyebrows.

Ezekiel put his arm around Phoebe and Kelly laughed. "Well, well Ezekiel you dark horse you. We will speak later."

Phoebe could not wait for the service to be over to question Ezekiel about Kelly. They knew each other and seemed friendly?

Phoebe couldn't fight the uncomfortable feeling that Kelly was sitting behind her and judging her for being there with Ezekiel. In her opinion Kelly should be the one feeling guilty, not her. But then she remembered that Kelly was Erica's sister. What if Erica had said something to her about Phoebe's intention to marry rich?

Then Ezekiel would think she was a gold digger and ditch her just when she was getting so close to her goal.

She was in for a shock though, because after church, Theo and Ezekiel were shaking hands and talking chummy.

"Why don't you come back to our place for lunch?" Ezekiel was asking Theo and Kelly.

"Would love to," Kelly grinned, "I have not seen that place since I refurbished it."

Kelly was responsible for all of that luxury? Phoebe gasped. She was really good then. She now saw the connection without having to ask. Kelly was the talented designer who did Ezekiel's house. Then she remembered that he had said 'our' place and then felt warm all over—she liked the sound of that.

The dinner together was going remarkably well, Phoebe had to admit. They were dining on the patio overlooking the sea. Ezekiel had served more of his jambalaya rice and salad. He and Theo had prepped the food together, talking and laughing in the kitchen.

Kelly hardly spoke to Phoebe when they were gone. She was not very comfortable around her and Phoebe could understand why, so she didn't push. She didn't want to invite any confidences with Kelly and then have her asking her why she was in Cayman with Ezekiel. But she couldn't help staring at the little boy in fascination. He was supposed to be around two years old now. He was super-cute, with his pink rose bud mouth and his big bright hazel eyes.

When they were all seated together Theo and Kelly were very easy to be around. Their children were well behaved, but their little girl kept staring at Phoebe and she was tempted to ask the brat to stop contemplating her so hard—she tried to remember her name but couldn't.

Finally, she asked her in her friendliest voice, "what's your name again?"

"Thea," the little girl replied.

"Is there something on my face why you are looking at me so long?"

The little girl scrunched up her nose. "No, I was just wondering if you and Uncle Ezekiel are married."

Phoebe started fidgeting and thought— note to self — never question a child in public again; they have no tact or diplomacy.

"No we are not." Phoebe cleared her throat.

The conversation that had been going on around them stopped and everyone was listening in. Ezekiel had a big smile on his face and Kelly was looking on inquiringly.

Why don't you tell your child to mind her own business,

Phoebe felt like screaming at the grinning couple.

"So," Thea continued, "if you are not married to Uncle Ezekiel why are you two here together?"

"That's enough Thea," Theo said a warning in his voice. "I think this line of conversation comes under adult conversation."

Theo looked at Phoebe warmly. "Sorry about the questions. Our daughter is going through that stage where everybody's business is fair game."

Well bully for you, when she starts asking why the baby does not look like the two of you. Phoebe thought wildly.

Ezekiel laughed. "To your question Thea, I would marry her right now."

"Is that so?" Kelly asked interestedly.

"Oh yes," Ezekiel said easily not realizing that Phoebe was looking uncomfortable. Kelly knew all about her little stalking episode on Chris. And how she hadn't made any secret of the fact that she wanted to marry rich.

Phoebe could just see Kelly calling Ezekiel and warning him off. He would probably listen to her too, she was his designer and they seemed to have a good relationship. Drat it, she cursed in her mind.

She forced a smile on her face and looked somewhere in Kelly's direction. "People change and mature."

Kelly's eyebrows sprung up even higher at that, Phoebe could see her, in her mind's eye, telling Erica and talking about it.

Erica would tell her all her secrets and Kelly would tell Ezekiel that Phoebe was a gold-digger. All her dreams of being rich would be dashed.

Chapter Fifteen

They went to the party on a yacht that night; it was fairly pleasant. The women spoke about their children and babies and their charity work. The men gathered off to one side and spoke about fishing and property deals.

This was a group of Ezekiel's closest friends. She felt ridiculously young and gauche compared to them. The hosts were pleasant enough and the food was good. The women did try to include her in their chatter but she didn't know them. She felt detached from the whole conversation and found herself smiling vaguely at their jokes.

She was half listening to the old reggae songs from the 60's and she suddenly felt nostalgic. She could remember listening to these songs when her father played them on his LP record. She would lie in her bed and imagine that she was rich and far away from the world she lived in.

Somehow, the reality was not meeting up to her dreams. She still yearned for something more.

She heard Dobby Dobson's song 'The Loving Pauper' and for the first time the words resonated with her, she found herself thinking that the words were something that Charles would sing to her—now she couldn't stop thinking about him.

She had called him hurriedly before she left for the weekend and told him she would be out of the country and then hung up before he could answer. She found herself standing alone to one side of the boat, staring out at the darkness of the sea and hearing the sea lap against the expensive boat.

She felt a deep yearning for something—she had no idea what it was that she wanted but she felt lonely and unsettled. She came to the realization that she would probably feel this way forever, even if she married Ezekiel and was instantly rich. Maybe she was chronically unhappy, maybe it was something in her genes from her mother's side of the family.

She felt an arm around her and looked up jerkily. It was Ezekiel. He was standing beside her with a drink in his hand.

"You look unhappy, like you are on the verge of tears."

Phoebe sniffed. "I don't know what's wrong with me." Tears welled in her eyes.

"Do you want us to get out of here, go somewhere quiet and talk?"

Phoebe nodded. "Can we? We are some ways from shore."

Ezekiel squeezed her arm. "Give me five minutes."

He went on the upper deck and whispered to his friend and in a few moments they were heading for shore.

Phoebe had a fake smile plastered on her face when she was waving to the people who were commiserating with her for not feeling well.

When she was finally alone with Ezekiel he turned her around and looked searchingly in her face and then hugged her. They stood in the quiet night of the Barcadere Marina and hugged.

Phoebe burrowed herself in his strong arms hoping to calm the storms that were raging in her mind; he hugged her tightly, trying to be her anchor.

Then she started to sob because she saw Charles in her mind's eye with that carefree grin on his face and she knew that she would probably hurt him. She also knew that Ezekiel was far more invested in her than she deserved; she was confused and unsure of what to do.

He let her sob, then he dried her tears and they sat on one of the benches in the marina park, just staring off into the night.

He hugged her and she leaned her head on his shoulder, tendrils of her hair sneaked down the front of his shirt and he played with them.

"I thought parties are supposed to be happy." His voice was hoarse.

Phoebe giggled nervously. "They are, maybe I'm just not a happy person, maybe I'm incapable of enjoying myself."

Ezekiel swallowed. "Close your eyes and think about it, what is the one occasion in your life that when in that moment you wished it could last forever."

Phoebe closed her eyes and her mind could only conjure up that time when she kissed Charles. She wished she could kiss him forever, inhale his scent, and spend every day in his arms. She wasn't poor then or thinking about money. She hadn't been thinking or calculating, she had just felt light and free.

She took her head up from Ezekiel's shoulder, she couldn't tell him that. She put some distance between them on the bench and sighed.

He intertwined their hands together and squeezed them. "Your happiest time in your entire life till now was with

Charles Black?"

Phoebe gasped. "How'd you know...I mean what gave you that impression?"

Ezekiel grimaced. "A wild guess...the fact that I'm not totally oblivious to the happenings in your life. I know that I practically threw you two together with the car gift."

He stood. "I realize that you are conflicted Phoebe. I understand it on some level. I am jealous as hell but I understand it. As I said before, the ball is in your court."

He ran his fingers through his hair. "Let's go home and get some sleep. Both of us have a lot to think about."

Phoebe nodded dejectedly. "I am sorry for being a wet blanket and ruining your weekend."

"Being with you and having you being honest with me isn't a ruinous thing." His voice sounded raspy when he finally spoke.

Chapter Sixteen

When Ezekiel dropped her home on Sunday evening, he planted a kiss on her forehead.

"I will send your clothes over tomorrow," he told her. "Sleep well tonight. I will call you."

Phoebe stepped out of the car with her weekend bag and opened her gate. Charles was sitting on his verandah looking out into the night. He was on his guitar, strumming it softly. She paused on her walkway. Waiting for him to acknowledge her but he continued playing, ignoring her.

She went into the house and put down her weekend bag. Her parents were watching television in the hall.

"How was it?" her mother looked up at her smiling.

"Fine," Phoebe said dejectedly.

Nishta frowned. "You spent the weekend in Cayman and it was just fine?"

Phoebe nodded.

Her father was lying down in the long settee; he looked at

her with a wealth of sadness in his deep brown eyes.

"I think," he cleared his throat, "that a woman should not be with a man for profit. She should be with him for love through thick and thin." He pointed his thumb at Nishta. "It is hell living with a woman who doesn't love you for being you, and who nags you everyday to change yourself."

He sat up straighter. "Don't let her poison you Phoebe and make that man unhappy. No matter how rich or poor a man is, a marriage becomes a prison if you aren't happy. In the process you too will be unhappy."

"How dare you?" Nishta growled. "There has never been any thick but lots of thin in this marriage. I am sick and tired of you only thinking that we should be happy in this ugly place with no money and hardly any food. Struggling together is not attractive, and more so after twenty or more years.

You know what Phoebe," Nishta spun around and looked at Phoebe, "poverty is not the only bad thing, it's lack of ambition. When you are with a man who is only content to do the same thing over and over with no reward, your life is doomed."

Phoebe groaned. They would be at it all night after this. Her father was usually nag averse. He said nothing to upset Nishta, but tonight he must have been very upset to be this confrontational.

Phoebe sat on her bed. She could hear the faint strumming of the guitar next door through her mother's shouting and the television sounds.

She hauled on her tracksuit bottom and a tank top and folded with care the expensive maxi dress that she had worn back.

She suddenly felt hungry. She had picked at her food earlier at lunch with Ezekiel. She hadn't been relaxed or comfortable with him after Saturday night. He had looked pensive after they got home and Phoebe had been feeling guilty. She had gone to her room and sat on the balcony for hours, unable to sleep.

She wouldn't dare go scrounging around in the kitchen now though. She didn't want to be a part of her parents' argument.

Phoebe went onto the veranda and looked over at Charles' veranda and realized that she had never been over to his house. She knew it was his uncle's house and that his uncle worked in another parish and only visited the place occasionally.

She made up her mind to go over there, despite the hostility she could feel coming off Charles in waves.

When she approached the veranda she realized that the house was in much better condition than the one she lived in. It was in white and there was no peeling paint anywhere. Even the yard was better. The grass was actually green and looked well cared for.

"So the grass really is greener on the other side," Phoebe said walking up to the veranda and sat beside Charles on the steps.

He looked over at her; his eyes were glistening in the moonlight. "You should tell me," he said taking off his guitar and setting it at his feet. "Where did you go this weekend with your rich lover?"

"He isn't my lover," Phoebe said through clenched teeth, "and you and I aren't together. You have no right to ask me that."

"Fair enough," Charles nodded. "Would you consider my advice then, as a friend?"

Phoebe shrugged. "Go ahead."

"Give him back his car, stop taking his gifts. Stop using

him. They have a name for women like you."

"Stop it!" Phoebe exclaimed weakly.

Just then Charles' friend, Howie, rode up on his bike.

"Hey Charlie, I got your order here." He took a paper bag from out of his knapsack. "Oh hi Phoebe."

"Hey." Phoebe waved. Charles went for his food and said goodbye to Howie.

"I was hungry," he explained to Phoebe. "I haven't eaten since you called and told me you were leaving the country. I just knew that you had gone off with that sugar daddy of yours and I couldn't bear to see the sight of food after that."

He took out two burgers. "Want one?"

Phoebe was busy feeling all warm inside. She had thought about him too but she was not about to tell him that.

"It's chicken," he said handing it to her.

"Oh thanks." Phoebe took it from him eagerly. "I was feeling hungry, picked around my lunch."

Charles snorted. "Must be your conscience acting over time." He then bit into his burger.

He wolfed it down in the time that Phoebe took to eat half of hers and then he dug into the paper bag for fries.

"So, how was your foreign trip?" He asked, a jealous glint in his eye.

"I went to Cayman," Phoebe replied enjoying her burger.

"Oh," Charles grimaced, "had sex on the beach?"

"Nooo," Phoebe said annoyed, "I told you already, I didn't have sex with him."

"But you would have, if he pushed you," Charles said knowingly, "you would have given up your prized virginity because he's rich and powerful and just what you have always fantasized about."

Phoebe closed her eyes. Would she or wouldn't she? She probably would have. Ezekiel's kiss was electrifying. There was a whole host of maturity and experience in that kiss. And he wanted to marry her. So in essence she would be sleeping with him because he had money and because she wanted the benefits of his wealth, just like bartering—my body, your house.

"That would make me a whore," she whispered to Charles, putting down her burger between them. "Sex in exchange for money is..." her voice trailed away.

She had a lost look in her eyes. "My mother has been pushing me to whore out myself to the highest bidder hasn't she?"

Charles took up the burger and asked. "Do you want this?"

"No." Phoebe wiped her mouth on a napkin and watched as he wolfed it down.

"I think," Charles said, "that it is convenient to blame your mother for your decisions but if you haven't realized it yet, Phoebe, you are near a quarter of a century years old. Your decisions are yours. You are the Christian, not Nishta. Didn't you say that Nishta thought going to church was for idiots? I think you can shake her influence if you want to, but you don't want to."

He wiped the corner of his mouth and then looked at her with a lopsided grin on his mouth. "What do you want Phoebe?"

Phoebe turned her confused eyes on him. "I don't want to be poor."

"And does the opposite of poor have to be stinking rich?" Charles asked, "can't it be just living comfortably? And does it have to involve a man? What about getting yourself out of poverty on your own merit?"

"Whoa," Phoebe stared at Charles aghast, "where is all of this coming from?"

"It is coming from someone," Charles said seriously, "who

genuinely wants to see you do well. It is not enough anymore to think that happiness is an outside job. I have feelings for you," he turned her chin around and smirked, "and I want you to be as beautiful on the inside as you are without. I really want that."

He leaned toward her and kissed her nose tip.

Phoebe leaned into him and initiated a deep soul searching kiss that ended when they heard a car coming up the road.

Charles pulled away from her, "maybe you should go. My self-control isn't really good right now."

Phoebe went back over to her house, a trembling mass of sensations with the biggest smile on her face.

Chapter Seventeen

She drove to work for the first time since getting her license. It was a good feeling, and she was even going to meet Tanya for lunch. They hadn't seen each other for weeks and Tanya had called her last night after she had feverishly replayed the kiss in her head.

She had concluded that she and Charles had chemistry, very strong chemistry but chemistry did not mean love. It only meant that they were sexually compatible.

Many persons who married for sexual compatibility alone were now divorced. She personally knew a few of them. On the other hand, many persons who married for practicality were still married; she knew a few of those too.

Her whole family, by her mother's side, married for practicality. Her own grandparents were an arranged marriage. Her aunts all married men they were arranged to marry from birth.

Her mother was the only defiant one out of the lot and look

at her now—miserable and unhappy. There was something wrong with choosing a partner based on sexual compatibility. Phoebe had eventually worked out that probably that was what her mother, in her limited way, was telling her.

Phoebe went through work on autopilot until lunchtime when she met up with Tanya at Ballard's cafe. They served reasonably priced lunches to the surrounding business places and were a popular spot for young professionals to hang out.

Tanya was already seated in a corner booth.

"Hey stranger," she said when Phoebe sat down. "Are cell phones not a modern convenient way to call the people in your life?"

Phoebe looked at her friend and smirked. "Ditto."

Tanya flushed. "Well, I've been busy lately. I have lots going on. My mother is pregnant."

Phoebe whistled, "Isn't she like in her fifties?"

"Nope," Tanya said looking cornered, "she's in her early forties. My mother had me when she was a teenager."

"Ah," Phoebe nodded. "So what has you so upset?"

"If I were to get married and have children in the next year or two, the relationships would be awkward."

Phoebe laughed. "It won't matter, trust me. I wish I had a brother or sister, then my mother wouldn't have invested all her attention in me."

Tanya shuddered. "This means I'm not going to be an only child anymore. I won't be my Daddy's little girl anymore. Suppose the baby is a girl?"

Phoebe laughed. "You are too old to be Daddy's little girl."

Tanya grinned. "I'll always be my Daddy's girl! Hope the new addition is a boy though."

They ordered lunch—Tanya her regular jerk chicken burger and Phoebe her regular red peas soup. Whenever they met up they never changed their orders and they looked at each other and smiled.

"So what's up with you?"

"I'm seeing two guys." Phoebe blurted out looking around furtively.

"What?" Tanya asked stunned, "which two?"

"Ezekiel Hoppings and Charles Black."

"What in the world are you doing?" Tanya whispered.

"Help me Tannie please…" Phoebe sighed, "decide for me; put me out of my misery."

"I thought Charles Black wasn't an option, he's poor. Then again I thought Ezekiel Hoppings wasn't an option either, he's ugly."

"Forget that," Phoebe said looking pained, "I was naive and stupid to say those things. People can't be judged solely on looks and finances."

Tanya opened her mouth in shock. "Who are you and what have you done to Phoebe?"

The waiter carried the food and there was a little pause as Tanya contemplated her friend.

"Stupid Phoebe is dead. New Phoebe is confused." Phoebe took a sip of her soup.

Tanya looked at her burger and said, "I think I am in an alternate reality."

"I'm serious." Phoebe wiped her mouth delicately.

"Well if you are serious let's tabulate the pros and cons." Tanya rummaged in her bag and pulled out her notepad. It had the logo for the pharmacy where she worked as a pharmacist.

She drew up two columns Charles and Ezekiel. "Let's see," she scribbled under each line pros and cons.

"Okay go." She looked up at Phoebe with her notepad in hand and a quizzical look on her face; she looked like she was going to take a test.

Phoebe giggled. "Well, Charles is a Christian, handsome, charming, happy go lucky, always around, patient, kind, wise, sympathetic. Did I say handsome?"

"Yes." Tanya scribbled rapidly under the pros for Charles.

"Cons, well he's not ambitious, he's poor, only owns a bike, too friendly and giving, loves his friends too much, finds a song to fit every situation and psychoanalyzes the daylights out of me."

"Seriously." Tanya stopped scribbling, "too many of those reasons are not cons."

Phoebe shrugged, "oh and under pros for Charles you can put very high sexual chemistry."

Tanya put the notebook down and exhaled. "Dish it out sista! How'd you know that?"

"When we kiss I can feel electricity." Phoebe said dreamily.

Tanya laughed. "That's it—just kissing?"

Phoebe nodded.

"Well, let's go for pros with Ezekiel."

"He's cultured and confident, even with those scars, he's not self conscious, he's powerful, has a nice 'bod,' he has a good sense of humor and is knowledgeable about almost everything. He reads widely, he's sympathetic and kind, he's rich, has the most amazing residences, bought me a car and a wardrobe full of clothes, which by the way can't hold in my closet at home. I may have to give you some, oh and he is heavily into charity work."

Tanya stopped scribbling. "I say go for Ezekiel."

"I haven't even told you the cons yet." Phoebe said sipping on her soup.

"Okay, I guess it's fair," Tanya said taking up her notepad again. "But I see benefits for myself with this one so I am biased."

"He has these ugly scars," Phoebe said, "and that broken

nose thing. His eyes are beautiful and caring though. I have never found a man's eyes to be that beautiful before."

Tanya cleared her throat. "That's too much to write. Continue with the cons."

"He's fifteen years older than me. By the way, next month is my birthday. Don't forget this year."

Tanya nodded. "I only forgot last year because I was doing my exams."

"Fair enough. Oh, he's always flitting from one country to another, and busy all the time."

Tanya scribbled down busy/no attention on her paper.

"And his friends are boring," Phoebe rummaged in her bag, "and he's not a music lover. I realized since recently that I want a man who loves music."

"A man who loves art, respects the spirit world and thinks with his heart..." Tanya started crooning India Arie's song.

"Well, art is a given for Ezekiel. I've seen some really nice pieces in his home. Guess who designed his Cayman house?"

Tanya put down the notepad and bit into her burger. "Cayman...hmm...Kelly Palmer."

"How'd you know?" Phoebe asked.

"I think she designed his house in Jamaica too. I remember some talk about that couple years ago. People were clamoring to find out more about him and they were hounding Kelly because she was in his intimate circle of friends."

"Oh," Phoebe said, "I hadn't noticed anything about him except that he isn't attractive, he comes to church occasionally and sits at the back and slips out before the service is done."

"Me too," Tanya said, "anyways, based on your list for both, I say choose the one which makes your heart beat the hardest. Who you can't imagine taking another breath if you can't see them, the one who appeals to both your mind and your body."

"That's romantic rubbish," Phoebe snorted, "but on a scale of sexual chemistry with Charles being the highest, I'd put Ezekiel not far behind. As a matter of fact, extremely close, almost a tie. And he does appeal to my mind."

"You kissed him too?" Tanya squealed.

A piece of lettuce was on her front teeth and Phoebe laughed. "I guess I'm interesting now, huh?"

"You've always been interesting," Tanya said. "Maybe you should introduce me to one of them. They both sound good on paper. I could take one off your hands and then your choice would be clear because frankly Phoebe your cons for both guys are not that bad."

*****

Tanya was right, Phoebe concluded, but she didn't want to give up either of them at this point. She was packing up to leave for work when Ezekiel called her.

"Hey, Phoebe."

"Hey," Phoebe responded, feeling warm and awkward at the same time.

"Would you like to play hostess at a dinner party for me tomorrow evening? It is a small affair. I invited a few of my business associates and their wives to dinner. They're associated with a new charity I recently set up in Jamaica."

"What?" Phoebe squealed, "I can't make small talk and pretend with strange people!" She sat down hard in her office chair.

"You'll do fine," Ezekiel chuckled, "these are people who aren't afraid to give back some of their wealth to the less fortunate. They are easy to talk to, trust me, and they have a deep passion for making their country better."

"But..." she stammered.

"No 'buts' Phoebe," Ezekiel said gently. "You have to start sometime."

Phoebe digested that piece of information and groaned. He was not playing fair. Ezekiel wasn't going to give her any space to make up her mind about him alone.

"Okay, I'll do it," she said feeling burdened all over again.

"Well, see you tomorrow," he said gently and hung up the phone.

*****

"So, she said yes." Sonia was sitting across from him with a cross look on her face.

"That's right," Ezekiel said smiling. "If you hadn't suggested that I needed a hostess for this party, I would have just hosted it alone, but Phoebe will manage it."

"She is from Flatbush Scheme," Sonia said scornfully, "she probably doesn't know how to use the place settings."

"Then we'll dine buffet style," Ezekiel shrugged.

"What's with you and this girl?" Sonia asked exasperatedly. "I have never seen you so...so...dreamy looking and off kilter. You are really taking this 'charity begins at home' saying too far."

"I love her," Ezekiel said simply, "I can't explain it. Frankly, I have never felt this way before."

"I can explain it," Sonia said getting up and pacing, "you are going through a mid-life crisis. You feel jaded and confused with your jetting to different places every other week. Take a vacation. Relax. Stop obsessing about her. So she's young and pretty, but clearly you can see that she is after your money."

Ezekiel laughed. "I have a lot of it. I don't mind that she wants financial security. I'm banking on just that for her to say yes when I officially propose to her."

"You have gone mad," Sonia shook her head at him, "and you are thinking with your lower brain."

Ezekiel reclined in his chair and swiveled to gaze at the scenery. He could clearly see the beach from his study, its blue arms hugging and flirting with the rocks on the shore.

He wanted to shout at Sonia and tell her to get out of his office, but she was right. He had gone mad over Phoebe and couldn't wait to make her his.

He wanted her in his bed, in his home and in his life.

Several times he was tempted to act possessive and jealous over her. He had been sputtering mad when she had all but admitted that her happiest moments were with Charles Black.

He had to restrain himself from ruining Charles Black for daring to steal his woman. He had thought about it several times, but he had become lucid enough in his thoughts to know that nothing good could ever come from treating people as possessions.

He had been on the verge of acting like King David in the Bible, but remembered that his little act of self-indulgence had caused generations of family problems.

He had purposed in his heart that he would honor God in his approach to pursuing Phoebe. But he also had a steely determination that he would have her.

"There you go, zoning out on me again," Sonia said exasperatedly.

"Ah." Ezekiel swiveled back his chair around to face her and fanned her to sit down. "I don't care where Phoebe is from, or that she's after my money. I have a sneaking fear that I love her enough for both of us and that is enough for me."

Sonia grimaced at this statement. She really needed to pay Phoebe Bridge a visit in Flatbush Scheme and sort this out once and for all.

Chapter Eighteen

When Phoebe arrived home from work, a blue BMW was parked in the space she usually parked her car; she parked behind it intrigued. The front door of her house was wide open, but she couldn't see into its dim interior. She walked swiftly up the walkway and entered the house and there was Sonia Beaumont, sitting pretty on her mother's faded red velvet settee. Her mother was sitting across from her with an awestruck look on her face.

"Phoebe this lady here says she has some business with you."

Phoebe looked at Sonia quizzically. "What do you want?"

Sonia was in an African print dress with brown and red patterns. Her hair was caught up in one and was very curly looking. She looked expensive and alien against the shabby background of her home.

"No need to sound hostile," Sonia said graciously. "I came by to talk to you."

"You and I have nothing to say to each other." Phoebe said playing with her car keys.

"But we do," Sonia said unhurriedly. She reached into her brown tote bag and pulled out a checkbook. "What will it take for you to leave Ezekiel alone?"

She had her pen poised over the checkbook, looking at Phoebe enquiringly.

Nishta gasped, she had been looking at both of them quietly during the exchange and she could feel the hostility in the air.

"You can't buy me off," Phoebe said sitting down across from Sonia and beside her mother who was wide-eyed with anticipation. "I'm not stupid. If you are so eager to get rid of me, you must be running scared."

Nishta grunted. "That's right, she must be scared. But I say let's start the bargaining at ten million dollars."

"Mama," Phoebe said glancing at her mother, "are you out of your mind?"

Nishta shook her head, "money is money, she has it and she's offering it. Why not take it?"

"She wants me to leave Ezekiel alone," Phoebe said looking at Sonia.

"You don't love him you don't even like him," Sonia said to her earnestly. "I can write a check for ten million dollars as your mother said, and we'll never speak of this again."

"You hear that Phoebe," Nishta said, her voice high with anticipation "Take the money, there is a lot we can do with that money. We can leave this place, buy a car, and take a vacation. You can even have the freedom to go out with that poor guy next door without worrying about money."

Phoebe worried her lip and thought about it. It was tempting to send Sonia away and act affronted that she wouldn't take the money because she was above such bribery, but deep inside she knew she wasn't that noble and as her mother said, money was money. But there was something about Ezekiel that she liked and she found that she didn't want to cut him out of her life just like that.

Contrary to what Sonia said she did like him. He was an acquired taste and the more time she spent around him the more necessary he was beginning to be in her life. She was not that cold-blooded to barter away her bourgeoning feelings for Ezekiel for ten million dollars. She looked across at Nishta who was practically salivating at the thought of the money.

Phoebe shook her head. "I can't take your money." She looked balefully at Sonia. "I won't be leaving Ezekiel alone. I'm going to host a dinner party for him tomorrow."

Sonia hissed her teeth. "Are you nuts?"

"Yes Phoebe, are you crazy?" Nishta piped in. "Maybe she wants more...fifteen million maybe?" Nishta asked Sonia craftily.

Sonia was poised to write again. "So is that it? Fifteen million? Will that be enough for you to leave Ezekiel alone?"

Phoebe shook her head. "No. "

"Phoebe!" Nishta squealed.

Sonia closed her checkbook. "Maybe you need some time to think about it then? My offer will not be opened forever." She handed a business card to Phoebe. "Call me when you have made up your mind."

Phoebe stared at the business card long after Sonia had left.

Nishta was beside herself highlighting how they could spend the money. Phoebe didn't hear a word; her hands were trembling with the business card.

"Maybe you don't think we are poor enough then," Nishta said huffily.

Phoebe's thoughts were echoing the same refrain. She looked at Sonia Beaumont's fancily designed business card with its gold engraving of her name and then tore it up slowly.

She was uneasy with bribes; had always been.

Nishta's eyes widened after each tear, her lips were trembling with shock. "Phoebe," she whispered, "what are you doing?"

Phoebe looked at her mother and patted her knee, "what does it profit a man if he gains this whole world and lose his own soul. That was a soulless bargain Mama."

*****

The dinner party for Ezekiel was a smashing success. They dined buffet style and even though at first Phoebe was overawed at the atmosphere and the guests, she relaxed when she remembered the words Ezekiel had whispered in her ear earlier. "You'll be fine, they are just people who happen to have some extra money that they are eager to give away to make a difference in the society they live. This makes them a good crowd. Relax."

She had relaxed after the first ten minutes and was enjoying the company. They were a younger set of people; one girl was even the same age as Phoebe, the first wife of a senator who was head over heels in love with her husband. Her husband was a very rotund man with a heavily whiskered face. Phoebe couldn't see the attraction but she could feel the love between them and she got a bit envious. Every few words from the girl's mouth were, 'honey says.' She wasn't especially pretty but was extremely vivacious. Her name was Rachel, and she was an Investment Banking Analyst.

"I love my job," she was telling Phoebe, "that's how I met my honey bunny. How'd you meet Ezekiel?" Her bright brown eyes were curious.

"Church," Phoebe said smiling.

"I didn't know Ezekiel goes to church," the girl gasped.

Phoebe nodded. "He does."

"So was it love at first sight?" Rachel was sipping at her cocktail and settling in for the romantic details.

Phoebe shrugged and just then Ezekiel sauntered over to them and put his arms around her. "It was for me."

Rachel smiled. "Awww, that's so sweet."

Ezekiel smiled. "I have loved Phoebe for a long time. Sometimes I feel as if I have loved her forever."

Rachel gasped. "Do I hear wedding bells for the most eligible bachelor in Jamaica?"

Ezekiel kissed a stunned Phoebe on her cheeks. "Stay tuned…"

He sauntered off to join a group of men who were beckoning to him; leaving a very shaken Phoebe staring off into space. Could she do it? Could she really marry Ezekiel? Would it be fair to him? Would it be fair to her?

She barely heard the conversation floating around her. Her mind was buzzing. She had really changed. In the past all she could think about was marrying rich but now when it was on the table, a fear deep down in her heart was overtaking her thoughts.

"How are you?" An older lady in a green dress with a boat collar was staring at her interestedly. Her hair was caught up in a loose bun and her eyes were bright and warm. Rachel had gone somewhere else and Phoebe hadn't even realized.

"I am fine." Phoebe looked at her curiously. She was dressed simply and had a humble air about her.

"I'm Carol," she held out her hands for Phoebe to shake, "Ezekiel's aunt." She stared at Phoebe assessingly. "Are you interested in charity work?"

Phoebe was still digesting the fact that Ezekiel had an aunt. "Uh...sure. I volunteer for the feeding program at our church. I had no idea Ezekiel had family here."

Carol chuckled. "He has a boatload of cousins and two aunts from his mother's side living in Jamaica. Most of the family lives in Kingston. I am the head of the charity organization Child Of Promise. Have you ever heard of it?"

Phoebe shook her head. "No."

"Well, Ezekiel started it ten years ago. He helps poor children through school: from basic school to university, even to the doctoral level. Many of them wouldn't have had easy access to educational opportunities because of their poverty. I think this latest charity is an extension of that."

Phoebe filed that information away and felt slightly ashamed that in her dreams of having great wealth she hadn't once thought about sharing it with someone else. All her dreams were of selfish indulgences.

Ezekiel's charity work put her to shame. He wasn't only rich but he cared. He had some purpose in his life; he took his stewardship of his wealth and his responsibility to the society in which he lived quite seriously.

He deserved somebody who would be a good compliment to him—not a mindless gold-digger. She chit-chatted with Carol for a few more minutes learning even more about Ezekiel, and the more she learned the more she felt like a shallow fraud.

*****

"That went well." Ezekiel turned to her in the marble foyer as the last guest departed. "I am so proud of you."

"Thank you," Phoebe smiled at him shyly, "I didn't do anything really. Your guests were really outgoing. That made it easier. And your aunt was extremely entertaining. She told me a lot about your childhood."

Ezekiel pulled her into his arms. "I have been wanting to do this all night." He bent his head and kissed her a soul searching kiss that had Phoebe's toes curling and the two of them heaving for breath. When he released her, they looked at each other.

Ezekiel was staring at her deeply. "Marry me Phoebe. I love you."

Phoebe opened her mouth and he put a finger over her lips.

"I don't want to hear no. I love you enough for both of us," he whispered.

He kissed her again; a soft kiss and he placed his forehead on hers. They looked into each other's eyes for a while.

"I just don't know what to say." Phoebe whispered.

"Say yes," Ezekiel whispered back.

"Can I think about it?" Phoebe cleared her throat.

Ezekiel straightened up. "Okay, but please don't leave me waiting too long for a response. I think I'll need time to set my business affairs in order and book myself into an asylum if you refuse."

Phoebe giggled nervously.

Chapter Nineteen

He called her everyday. He proposed everyday. For one full week, she was bombarded by gifts and tokens. He sent her flowers at work and at home and gift baskets with exotic fruits.

For her birthday, he took her to Rock Face, an exclusive eatery that was located in a cave. Their table was situated in a bracket of stalactite and stalagmite rocks. The lighting was low and perfect, and violin music played while they ate. It was super romantic and he was appealing to her every sense. It was obvious Ezekiel knew how to woo a woman. Phoebe found herself feeling dizzy after each outing with him, especially after he kissed her. His kisses were long and had her yearning for more.

The next day when she got back from her romantic whirlwind dinner and turned on her phone she was bombarded with messages from Tanya, Erica, and Charles.

She had been deliberately trying to avoid Charles. She

found herself tiptoeing down her walkway in the mornings, watching to see if his bike was at the front of his house before she dashed to her car. She was feeling all guilty and sneaky rolled into one.

Today she called him, pressing his phone numbers gingerly, wishing he wouldn't pick up. But it seemed as if Charles was sitting and waiting for her to call; as soon as the phone rang he answered.

"I have something to show you later," he said, no hint in his voice that she had been ignoring him.

"Oh," Phoebe responded cautiously, "what is it?"

"Later after work, I'll show you." He had a grin in his voice.

"Okay." Phoebe relaxed.

"By the way, happy belated birthday Phoebe," he said light heartedly. "I didn't hear from you yesterday, I suppose you were out with your rich friend."

Phoebe was silent.

"Okay, I promised myself I wouldn't say a thing." Charles sighed. "See you later."

Phoebe hung up and sat on her bed.

She dialed Tanya's number and a sleepy Tanya came on the line.

"I thought you were going walking with your friends this morning," Phoebe said cheerfully.

"It rained last night," Tanya said grumpily, "so we put it off till in the evening. Happy belated birthday. How are things going? You've been so busy these days."

Phoebe gave her a run down of how she was spending her time and how Ezekiel had proposed to her.

Tanya was silent for a while. "If a man says he loves you enough for both of you, you should take him…"

Phoebe hung up the phone from Tanya and dialed Erica's

number.

Erica answered giggling. "Stop it." She was talking to someone in the background. Phoebe could imagine her and Caleb playing and enjoying their time together, she really wanted that for herself—to be comfortable with a man, like Caleb and Erica were. Theirs was the genuine thing.

"Sorry to call at this hour," Phoebe said smiling, "but you two always seem to be at it."

Erica giggled again and then said in the phone, "Phoebe Bridge, I baked a cake for your birthday and I have a present for you, when I called you yesterday you were nowhere to be found."

"I went out," Phoebe said cautiously.

"Oh, Charles took you out?" Erica asked suddenly sounding serious.

"No," Phoebe sighed, "long story, but Ezekiel asked me to marry him."

Erica gasped. "Don't do it Pheebs, it would be like unholy matrimony. You marrying him for money; him marrying you because of your looks."

"It's not like that," Phoebe sighed, "I genuinely like Ezekiel and he loves me."

"What about Charles huh?" Erica asked, "I like him for you."

"I know," Phoebe said, "but didn't you hear, Ezekiel loves me. Love trumps like."

Erica was silent for a while. "Don't you dare settle with Ezekiel just because of money. I want you to be happy and comfortable in your mind and in your relationship. That means when you walk down that aisle you should be a hundred percent sure that you are doing the right thing. No settling, you hear me?"

Phoebe sighed, "I hear you. We'll talk later."

"Yes," Erica said readily, "I'll drop off your present on my way to work later this morning, will leave it with your Mom. And if you come to church this Sabbath we'll talk, okay."

"Okay." Phoebe hung up the phone.

*****

As soon as Phoebe got home from work that day, she called Charles. She couldn't wait to see what he had to show her. He had seemed so excited over the phone.

"I'm outside," Charles said importantly, a tinge of excitement in his voice.

When Phoebe went outside she saw him waving from a battered old car with multi-colored bodywork. It reminded her of her gate, and she burst out laughing.

"Charles what's this?" she asked, heading toward him.

"I bought it two days ago," Charles said laughing, "I also enrolled in some managerial courses at the hospitality college. I am a young man on the rise for you."

Phoebe looked at him aghast. "Are you serious?"

"Yes." Charles came out of the car and had to slam it several times before the door finally closed. "I know you loved that car that Ezekiel gave to you and I thought why not make an effort to help you to make the decision to ditch him."

Phoebe closed her eyes and then opened them again. "You expect me to drive this junk pile to work instead of that?" She pointed to her car.

Charles shrugged. "I'll fix up this old Ford Escort. I'm thinking black will make a nice color. The boys and I will work on it all the time, and in no time it will look good. You'll see."

"So how will you find time for that while going to

hospitality school?" Phoebe asked squinting at him. "And working? And playing gigs on the weekends?"

"It's all about time management," Charles grimaced, "that's the name of one of my first classes by the way. With time management you can't go wrong."

Phoebe shook her head. "I don't know if I want you to put yourself through that just for me."

Charles laughed. "I'm not just doing it just for you, Phoebe. I am also doing it for me. You know, you made me realize that I can't just continue drifting with the tide. I have to have some goals or one day I might just find myself to be a middle-aged drifter sitting on my uncle's veranda pondering where did it all go wrong."

Phoebe clapped her hands in glee. "So I made a difference didn't I?"

"Yup," Charles grinned, "and I'm also hoping that you'll see that I'm a good prospect in the competition for your fair hand."

Phoebe giggled and then she couldn't stop. "You sound like an English radio drama."

Charles laughed with her, and then jiggled his keys. "Want to go for dinner? Consider this your birthday dinner. Since you went out with Mr. Rich Man last night, tonight I want to show you what you were missing with the new and upcoming Charles Black."

He yanked open the car door on the driver's side and made a swooping motion for Phoebe to get in.

"Sorry about the other side. Apparently it can't be opened, so you'll have to come through here."

Phoebe peered into the car and scowled, "the seats look like vermin could live in them."

Charles grinned. "I personally dusted them out with my cleanest house broom."

"Oh Lord," Phoebe groaned, "wait here, I am going to put on pants and go for my Lysol."

She ran inside and came back in army fatigues and a Lysol in hand. "Okay 'new and upcoming Charles Black.' I am here to be taken to dinner."

*****

Charles took her to Burger Joint, a sports lounge where people could eat, sit around and watch television, or play their own games. There were several pool tables but most of them were occupied. They feasted on huge burgers while they watched reruns of the Diamond League Athletics meet on television.

Earlier Charles had whipped out a game of Scrabble from the back seat of his car—the plastic was still covering the box.

He cleared his throat "Well, I started studying the dictionary to keep up with you..."

Phoebe grinned. He had such an earnest expression on his face. "You know Charles, you are something else."

"Well, I know you like this word game and as part of my 'new upcoming image', I am now a Scrabble player."

"Okay, 'new up and coming Charles'," Phoebe laughed, "I'll teach you how to play."

They played for two hours, Charles got the hang of the game and he managed to play an impressive word or two. Phoebe found herself looking at him and simply smiling at times.

He was serious enough about her to want to change his life. But on the other hand, Ezekiel was serious enough to want to marry her as well, and was waiting for an answer.

On their way home, the car started to sputter.

Charles kept apologizing for it and Phoebe kept laughing.

"You know Charles," Phoebe kissed him on the cheeks. "I have never in my entire life laughed so much in one evening." She gave him her Lysol. "Keep this for your car seat. Goodnight."

"Goodnight," Charles whispered, a look of devotion crossing his face. "I love you." He whispered when she was out of earshot. He was just as unsure about her now as he ever was.

He didn't even know if he was winning in this imaginary war for Phoebe's affection. Did she just find him to be an amusing guy who she could laugh with; was she even thinking of him seriously?

"Drat it." He kicked his car, wheeled and went slowly up the walkway to his house.

Chapter Twenty

Decisions, decisions, decisions. Phoebe sat cross-legged in the middle of her bed and contemplated her life. It had been two weeks since her birthday: She had played Scrabble with Charles a couple of days and had dinner with Ezekiel at his place a couple of days. Hung out with Tanya one evening and went to Erica's and Caleb's newly refurbished home on another.

Everybody had an opinion about her life.

Her mother constantly pushed her to call Sonia Beaumont and accept her bribe. "What are you waiting for Phoebe? Do it. I taped up back her business card. I found it where you tossed it in the trash."

Her father was deafeningly silent with his disapproving stares. Yesterday she heard him grumbling that he was "not pleased with all these goings on," after he came down from the roof he had finally managed to fix.

Charles kept pestering her to give back the car saying, "It is a symbol of whoredom." He actually played that in Scrabble one night and he had looked at her and pointedly said, "It is God telling you something."

Ezekiel wanted her to marry him. "Marry me Phoebe," he said with heartfelt tones, "I know we will be happy together. I can give you all that your heart desires."

Erica firmly believed that Charles was the one.

Tanya believed Ezekiel was the one.

Her mother believed anyone with money was the one.

What did Phoebe believe? Where did she stand?

Phoebe stared at her wall, there was a stain there from a mosquito she had killed three nights ago and hadn't bothered to wipe away the evidence.

What did Phoebe want to do? She stared at herself in the mirror and thought about that poem by Robert Frost, The Road Not Taken. They had forced her to memorize the poem in her high school literature class, now the words were reeling in her head:

Two roads diverged in a yellow wood,

And sorry I could not travel both,

And be one traveler, long I stood.

Well not stood, Phoebe realized. She was actually sitting and contemplating her options: she could marry Ezekiel and live on easy street; she could let Ezekiel down gently and give a relationship with Charles a go, or she could do as Charles said: be independent and go about her daily life and be content with what she had.

She worried her bottom lip between her teeth and kept staring at the blank wall until she dozed off into a troubled sleep. She didn't know why she suddenly woke up in the night, it could be the mosquito that was constantly zinging past her ears but she got up groggily and reached for her Bible and sat down with it.

Over the past few months, she had hardly prayed. Maybe

she had dashed a line or two of well-rehearsed drivel to God, but she definitely hadn't been reading the word. She had been so busy with her life and her problems and her poverty that she had no space for anything else, least of all God: her maker, the only person who had the Phoebe manual, and the only one who could solve the Phoebe problem.

And just like that Phoebe realized that all this time, she had been so self-centered, so caught up in her situation, so focused on everything that made her unhappy that she hadn't been focusing on the only solution.

She turned to Matthew 6 as if she was compelled to do so and read through the whole chapter prayerfully. When she read verse 19 she winced. It said, "lay not up for yourselves treasures upon earth, where moth and rust doth corrupt, and where thieves break through and steal."

Verse 24 said, "Ye cannot serve God and money," verse 31-33, "Therefore take no thought, saying, What shall we eat? Or, What shall we drink? or, Wherewithal shall we be clothed? (For after all these things do the Gentiles seek:) for your heavenly Father knoweth that ye have need of all these things. But seek ye first the kingdom of God, and his righteousness; and all these things shall be added unto you."

Phoebe had read this before, had heard it in church, had even participated in Bible study classes where this was read, but for the first time she understood it. For the first time in her entire life the concept was made plain.

Her attitude for the past few years was so opposed to this concept that she gasped with the enormity of it. And to think she had called herself a Christian.

Suddenly she saw, that her attitude to people, her attitude to both Charles and Ezekiel was wrong.

Her attitude to God was wrong.

Everything was just plain wrong.

It was a hard pill to swallow, and regret and recriminations roiled within her. How could she have been so one-track minded and blind? The reason why she was so unhappy was because she was so inwardly focused and self-centered.

All this time her only option was to seek God first. All other things would be added according to his will.

She concluded that God had been good to her; she was not nearly as poor as she could be. She had a job, she ate dinner every night, she had a church family and she did have friends who stuck with her despite her bad attitude.

She got off the bed feeling as if a huge burden was on her back. She wanted to change so badly. She wanted that peace that only God could give.

She fell to her knees and asked God for his forgiveness. Never in all her days did she feel such a deep regret about herself and her attitude toward life.

When she got up from her knees she had to look in her mirror to see if she had changed any at all, because she just felt lighter and free.

Chapter Twenty-One

Phoebe couldn't wait to go to church that Sabbath. The air just seemed fresher and the grass looked greener.

She had started packing the clothes that Ezekiel had bought for her to return them to him, so she wore a purple skirt suit that had seen better days. She was singing, and was so lighthearted that both her parents were looking at her strangely.

"So you've finally made up your mind about that rich man." Her mother clapped her hand gleefully.

Phoebe shook her head and looked at her mother compassionately, "Mama."

"Yes," Nishta answered tenderly.

"You need Jesus in your life," Phoebe said gently, "not money."

Nishta gasped. "Have you gone crazy?"

"Only crazy for Jesus." Phoebe said happily.

Phoebe's father was lounging in his chair when he heard the conversation and he looked at Phoebe gleefully. "That's my girl! I'm coming to church with you."

Phoebe shook her head. "You need Jesus too."

Her father got up eagerly. "We all need Jesus!"

Nishta had her hand on her head. "Jesus can't pay the bills! Jesus can't buy food." She moaned in agony.

Phoebe laughed. "He can and he has. Count your blessings Mama and you'll not be so miserable. You have a roof over your head, a long suffering husband, a daughter who has come to her senses...see you both later." She took up her umbrella and left the house.

When she arrived at church, the ushers greeted her at the door. "A warm welcome, Sister Phoebe. We haven't seen you in a while."

Phoebe grinned. "I was all over the place with the Perfect Number band. I am thinking that you'll be seeing a lot more of me now."

She went to sit beside Erica and Caleb who were wearing matching colors.

"The married madness has started," she whispered to them both.

Caleb grinned and Erica pinched her.

"You look different today Phoebe," Erica whispered, "really peaceful, like something for you has clicked into place."

"It has," Phoebe said hugging Erica sideways. "I have made up my mind about all of this madness."

"It's Charles, isn't it?" Erica squealed in delight, and then covered her mouth when the people before them turned around to look.

Phoebe smiled peacefully. "You'll know soon enough."

"I can't stand suspense," Erica said peeved. "Just tell me

and done."

"Nope." Phoebe grinned.

"I think it's the rich guy," Caleb said, "Phoebe has expensive taste. Remember the first thing she asked me that night, when I first saw you two, was 'where's your car?'"

Phoebe closed her eyes and blushed. "I am so sorry about that Caleb. I can only say that I was operating from an unconverted heart. But since then I have made it right with God. I am sorry I attacked you so aggressively in the parking lot that night."

Erica was staring at her wide-eyed. "Bless my soul! I have lived to see the day."

Phoebe fanned her off. "I am still a work-in-progress, thank God for Jesus."

Caleb grinned. "You are long forgiven Phoebe. I knew that underneath all your tough talk was a vulnerable and lonely girl."

"Awww," Erica said hugging Phoebe to her, "ma baby has grown up."

"Stop it," Phoebe hissed. "There's Hyacinth Donahue giving us the evil eye."

Erica laughed and wiped her eyes. "I am tearing up for all sorts of things these days."

"She's pregnant." Caleb offered sweetly.

"Tell the whole church, why don't you?" Erica whispered crossly.

"Somebody said pregnant?" Tanya sat beside them and asked loudly.

Erica sighed and moved closer to Caleb.

"Ah, congratulations." It was Phoebe's turn to hug Erica.

"You all have my permission to broadcast it to the church, but after church." Erica grinned still, wiping her wet eyes.

*****

It was a rousing sermon on the importance of tithing.

Pastor Brick quoted from Malachi 3:7-9: "Will a man, rob God yet you have robbed me, wherein have we robbed thee? In tithes and offerings."

He went on to espouse the lack of blessings that is the lot of many was a direct result of them robbing God.

The church was silent and pensive. Phoebe imagined that each person was doing his or her own soul-searching. Then her mind began to wander. She felt genuinely happy for Erica. She had truly never seen her friend look so content.

She looked over at Tanya who was clutching her Bible and searching through the texts.

Tanya genuinely loved God and she was fun to be around. Maybe she thought that Phoebe was too materialistic, and that's why she didn't ask her to attend any of her little girly meetings in the morning. Maybe she thought she would rub the other women the wrong way.

Suddenly Phoebe saw herself in the eyes of others. It was a miracle that Erica and Tanya even spoke to her. She was so obsessed with handsome men and material things and so fixated on poverty and all her lacks, that she must have been boring company.

She felt tears stinging her eyes. Becoming self-aware was no fun and as if she was viewing her life like a cinematic sequence she saw how utterly despicable and unapproachable she had been.

Though he really wanted to get her off his case, Chris Donahue had been the only one brave enough to publicly tell her to stop her rich-man-hunting. All the guys in church had shunned her. She cringed when she thought about how if a guy told her hello she would ask him how much he was worth and how much was in his bank account.

No wonder she had been unhappy. That kind of attitude

was rotten. She hadn't cared about people and caring about people was what Christianity was all about.

Phoebe felt well and truly down when church was over. She realized something else, when she went to the front door: other people greeted her friends effusively with warm hugs and handshakes but barely nodded at her, looking at her uncertainly as if she would explode at any moment.

Was she truly so standoffish, and why had she had the audacity to think that it was because people were jealous of her looks?

Phoebe and Tanya went home with Erica and Caleb to their newly refurbished place. It was gorgeous, and very different from the old house that was there before. They had built a second story onto the place to take advantage of the lovely views.

"So what is going to happen to Kelly's place?" Phoebe asked curiously as she sat outside on the balcony overlooking the bay, she could see the road below and a patch of greenery and of course the blue expanse of the sea. Up here, she could even hear it, lapping on the seashore.

"Well, I am thinking of just closing it up and sending someone there to clean it up every two weeks or so," Erica said. "I have no desire to go back there to live, when up here is so nice, and pretty soon I will be too taken up with baby issues to even care."

"Maybe I can housesit for you as long as Kelly and Theo won't mind," Phoebe offered, thinking what a good opportunity it would be to get away from her mother's constant nagging.

Erica looked at her and smiled. "That's a fabulous idea. They won't mind, and besides, I make the decisions regarding the house. I'll give you the keys when you are leaving."

"Cool," Tanya said, "I live near to Kelly's house. You can

come walking with the group in the mornings then. That's if you want to?"

"I probably will take you up on the offer," Phoebe nodded, "to hear exactly what it is you guys find to talk about in the mornings. I used to be so jealous of you people."

Tanya laughed. "That's funny, I thought that you'd found the whole thing boring, so I never extended an invitation. Besides, Flatbush Scheme is so far from our walking route."

"So what about Charles?" Erica asked eagerly, "won't he miss you when you move up to Kelly's place?"

Tanya grinned. "That shouldn't be a problem, she'll soon be marrying Ezekiel anyway."

Phoebe shrugged. "I prayed about it earnestly and I kept coming back to this decision."

"What is it?" Erica and Tanya asked in unison.

A stray wind whipped Phoebe's hair across her forehead and she pulled it back gently. "I have decided that I..."

Caleb came onto the verandah at the same time, with drinks. "Okay here we go ladies, callaloo juice, made with lemon and a dash of ginger."

"What's your decision?" Erica asked impatiently.

Caleb straightened up after placing the tray on the table, and sat down beside an impatient Erica.

Phoebe shrugged, "I have decided that..."

"This juice is extremely green," Tanya said interrupting Phoebe. "Is it naturally green or does it have coloring?"

Erica bristled. "Will the two of you stop talking? Phoebe is about to do the big reveal."

Tanya and Caleb grinned.

Phoebe sighed, "none of them."

"None of them," the three of them echoed.

Phoebe laughed. "Here's the thing: when you seek God first, you kind of leave the decision making to him. So I'm cutting all ties with both Charles and Ezekiel. I leave it to God and time."

"Ridiculous," Erica snapped. "Your decision can't be that you are not making a decision."

"Can I be kindly introduced to Charles?" Tanya asked excitedly, "I have liked him for a while now."

Phoebe nodded. "Sure, why not?"

Caleb hugged Erica to himself. "She's right you know. God and time."

Chapter Twenty-Two

Phoebe packed up the wardrobe that Ezekiel had bought for her and carried the bags one by one to the car. She would deliver them and the car to Ezekiel's place. She really hoped that she could get a ride back after she told him that she was refusing his proposal. She had already packed up her clothes and stuff and dumped them in the hall at Kelly's. Her mother had sat and watched her stony faced as she moved out.

"You are a stupid girl," Nishta sniffled, from the settee. She was suffering from a sinusitis attack and Phoebe was not sure if she was crying or if her eyes were streaming from sneezing. Nishta was looking miserable; her long gray streaked hair was plaited in two and she was in a washed out sari, which looked like it was once purple.

"After all the things I taught you." She sneezed and then blew her nose loudly.

Phoebe stood in front of her mother. "Mama, you are not too old to go and get yourself a job. You sit down day after day and watch your Hindi films and plot ways for me to win a rich husband—that's not healthy."

Nishta looked up on Phoebe, her eyes and nose tip red. "Who'll hire me, tell me that? I have a high school education and I have never worked before."

Phoebe kissed her on the forehead. "Don't worry about it, I'll find a job for you. Take care, I will drop by on Sunday, hopefully Tanya can drop me because I will have no car."

"Do you have to give back the car too?" Nishta asked incredulously. "It was a gift. It's an insult to give back a gift."

Phoebe laughed. "I am breaking up with the man. Keeping his gift wouldn't be classy. I'll buy myself a car someday. Stop worrying."

"You have really changed," Nishta said bitterly, "and I don't like it."

Phoebe grinned. "I am glad you see the changes too Mama, but I have a far way to go, and I like it."

When she left the house, she drove slowly out of Flatbush Scheme. Charles' car had not been in the driveway. She guessed he had either gone to school, to work or was playing at a gig.

The new and upcoming Charles was so busy these last three days that she hadn't even gotten the chance to tell him that they were no longer going to be neighbors. She'd try to call him tonight. Her concentration was now on the confrontation with Ezekiel that she was dreading; she had told him that she was coming to visit him today. He had sounded so delighted that Phoebe felt a pinch of guilt that she was going to tell him no to his proposal.

When she drove up to the security booth at his gate, the serious looking head of security grinned at her and opened the gate.

"Good to see you Miss Bridge."

"Nice to see you too Bryan." Phoebe smiled sweetly at him and drove through the front gate. Maybe this was her last time coming through the gates.

She remembered how impressed she had been when she had come through them the first time.

She was still impressed but this time she resolved that she wouldn't be so overwhelmed by the trappings of wealth that she could not tell Ezekiel goodbye.

She was striking out on her own. She wanted to be as beautiful on the inside as she knew she was on the outside, and if she accepted Ezekiel's proposal now she would never be truly comfortable in her own skin.

She admired him, she liked him a lot but she hadn't reached the love stage yet and though it was tempting to justify getting married to him because he loved her enough for both of them, she was not going to do that. She wasn't going to settle for material things and hope to be happy.

She wanted more than money or things. She wanted a man who she could be comfortable with, laugh with, have fun with and just be. Like what Erica had with Caleb. She parked beside a BMW that looked suspiciously like Sonia's and walked through a flower garden heading to the main house.

When she reached the main entrance the door was opened and Ezekiel's butler was there conferring with Sonia Beaumont. She was giving him some instruction or the other.

"Oh hello, Phoebe!" Sonia gave her a fake smile. "How nice of you to drop by."

Phoebe smiled at her, "I came to see Ezekiel not you."

"Oh he's in the study, madam. He's expecting you," the butler said to Phoebe, his eyes flicking over her appreciatively.

Phoebe passed the two of them and headed to Ezekiel's study, which was on the left wing of the house. She remembered feeling like she'd need a map the first time she had entered the place.

Now she knew where the study was, and was treated as if she belonged. She almost laughed out loud at the irony.

She was giving all of this up for what?

She ran through her mind the reasons again. If she vowed to love, honor and cherish Ezekiel, she'd be lying. Until she could stare any man in the face and mean those three things she wouldn't be getting married.

Ezekiel was standing at the window overlooking the pool area when she entered, from behind he had such a nice profile; he looked so handsome, tall and muscular.

He was dressed in jeans and a black polo shirt and even then he still exuded an air of dominance. Phoebe wondered idly if you had to be born with money to have that air or if it was just a result of Ezekiel's personality. He was not attractive in face but he was the most self-confident person she knew.

He turned and smiled at her when she entered.

She smiled back at him. "Hey."

"Hey," he said softly, his eyes traveled slowly over her outfit. She was wearing khaki shorts and a black singlet top and with sneakers, and she had her hair caught up in one.

She had no idea if she was going to have to walk all the way down from Bluffs Head after she told him her answer to his proposal was no, so she dressed for a walk.

"You look about seventeen," he said then he walked over to her and gave her a small peck on her cheek. "I really missed you these last three days. Where've you been?"

Phoebe eased herself out of his arms and started to pace. "Ezekiel, I like you."

Ezekiel looked concerned at her frantic pacing and said dryly, "Nothing good ever comes from a statement that is preceded by 'I like you', especially when it comes from the woman you love."

Phoebe stopped pacing and looked at him. He had his hands thrust in his pocket and he looked as if he was bracing for bad news.

"I can't marry you." Phoebe sighed and sat in the chair across from his desk. "My friend Erica says it would be like an unholy matrimony. I thought about it long and hard and I think she's right."

Ezekiel inhaled, sharply. A rush of pain had hit him somewhere in the region of his heart, and he could feel it spreading. He couldn't speak for a long while, and he leaned against the wall trying to get his composure.

I had expected this, he told himself. In the past few days he had even anticipated it, but he still felt stunned at the delivery.

"May I ask why?" His voice was hoarse, and his hands trembled a little. He was surprised that his voice was steady.

"Because," Phoebe looked around at him, "If I marry you now, I would be using you for this lifestyle. And when it starts to get stale, and I am tired of the amusements, I'd be unhappy. I'd want my freedom; I'd make you unhappy. Remember you told me that all you really want is somebody to love you for you?"

Ezekiel nodded. "I did say that, but I think I can handle it if you don't love me. Many relationships have been built on less."

"I know," Phoebe nodded, "at one time I even thought that I could do it. This may sound corny, but I want what my friend Erica has. I want mutual love and respect, friendship, just the ease of being with somebody who you can laugh and have fun with—love them for richer or poorer."

Ezekiel sighed long and deep, a dark cloud enveloping his head. "And you only have those things with Charles Black?"

Phoebe closed her eyes and swallowed. "I don't know if Charles is right for me either. He is fun to be around, and I like him a lot, but I don't love him either."

"You don't love him?" Ezekiel came to sit on the desk right in front of her. "But when we were in Cayman, you were crying over him."

Phoebe shook her head. "I think I was crying because I was so uneasy with myself and the decisions I was making. Charles is a great guy and there was this one song that I imagined he would sing to me...thinking back at it now it seems ridiculous."

She reached into the pocket of her shorts and removed the car keys. "I brought back the clothes and the car."

Ezekiel frowned, "Phoebe believe me when I say the car was really nothing for me to purchase. They are gifts to you—keep them."

"No," Phoebe looked him in the eyes. "I just won't be happy keeping them. I am turning over a new leaf. I am going the independence route; carving out my own destiny; not depending on anybody's wealth to validate myself."

Ezekiel looked at her, a soft look in his eye. "So let me get this straight. You are not refusing my proposal because you are taking up with Charles?"

Phoebe shook her head. "No."

"You are returning the car I gave you as a gift because you want to be independent?"

Phoebe nodded. "I do not want even the whisper of the word gold-digger near my name again. I have even moved out of my parents' house so that I can avoid my mother harassing me about marrying for money."

Ezekiel grinned. "So where are you living now?"

Phoebe looked at him puzzled. "I am breaking up with you...it shouldn't matter."

Ezekiel shrugged, "I know, but humor me. I can't switch off my love for you. You may have to give me some time to stop caring."

"Well," Phoebe worked her lips between her teeth. "I am staying at Kelly's house. Her sister Erica moved out. I am the new house sitter."

"Oh," Ezekiel's eyes gleamed, "can I call you sometime?"

"Well...er...sure," Phoebe said mistrusting his relaxed stance. "Can I get a lift back to Kelly's? I want to start unpacking my stuff."

"Sure, I'll ask George to drop you." Ezekiel walked her to the front door. Sonia was still there conferring with the butler. "Bye Phoebe."

"Bye Ezekiel," Phoebe said heading to the car, "I am sorry about all of this."

Ezekiel kissed her on her cheek. "It's okay. I'm happy that you are happy."

Chapter Twenty-Three

Sonia followed a grinning Ezekiel back inside his study.

"That was a short visit," she said looking at him with a question in her eyes.

"She came to break up with me—refused my marriage proposal," Ezekiel laughed, "took, back the car and the clothes."

Sonia gasped. "What? That's lovely...I mean, I am sorry. So why are you laughing?"

"Because I think I love her even more," Ezekiel said. "I realized something about Phoebe—she has integrity. And now I really, really want her to be my wife, and to be the mother of my children."

Sonia sighed in defeat. "I must admit I am surprised at her. When I offered her money to leave you alone, she refused."

"You did what?" Ezekiel asked surprised. "She did?" His mouth curved in a smile. "How much did you offer?"

"Her mother named the price my dear," Sonia said a

thoughtful look in her eyes. "I think the last figure was fifteen million."

Ezekiel hit the table in mirth. "Her mother sounds like a trip."

"She is," Sonia said seriously, "but what does this mean for us? You are still acting all moon-eyed over Phoebe."

"This means," Ezekiel said, "that I am going to do something that I have always vowed I would never do."

"What?" Sonia asked eagerly.

"I am going to call Dr. Neville Tate, the top cosmetic surgeon this side of the hemisphere and get my face redone. It's time for the beast to look special for his beauty."

"But...you swore you would never do cosmetic surgery," Sonia exclaimed aghast. "You said people have to accept you the way you are or don't accept you at all."

"I finally found a cause stronger than my need for surgery," Ezekiel said. "Phoebe gave up riches beyond her wildest dreams so that she can fix her inside issues. Well, I am going to give up my long held prejudices so that I can fix my outside issues."

"Can I borrow your butler for a party I am holding tomorrow evening," Sonia demanded realizing that she had no place in Ezekiel's love life. He was well and truly focused on Phoebe. "And when Little Miss Pretty waltzes in here as mistress of the house, I will not lift a finger to help her in your world."

Ezekiel shrugged. "Sonia you don't love me, you are on the rebound. I was a good candidate for you, lonely and pathetically grateful for your friendship when I am here. Be happy for me, why don't you? Like the good friend I know you are."

Sonia subsided in her chair. "Well, I did like to take care of you and it was a nice distraction after the divorce. Okay," she sighed, "I guess I owe Phoebe one, since she managed indirectly to get you to do surgery."

Ezekiel grinned. "That's the spirit."

*****

Ezekiel wasn't grinning when Sonia left his study. He was thinking about his past, how pathetically afraid he was of hospitals and surgery. When he was a boy of seventeen, he had allowed his fear to override the reasonable reassurances of his doctors that they could get his face back to its original look. He had resisted the very thought of surgery and it was this fear that had him looking at the phone reluctantly.

Tate would be overjoyed to hear from him. He had been hounding him for years to get his nose fixed and his scars removed. At a cocktail party a few years ago he had even told him that it would not take longer than six months for him to look normal again. "Your issues are easy to fix. I wish I could get my hands on you."

Ezekiel had laughed him off, but as he had said to Sonia just now, he was going to get it done for Phoebe. Her reasons for not marrying him had nothing to do with his looks or even about another man.

Her reason was because she needed self-improvement a whole new way to view life. He could make that choice too and meet her half way. He picked up the phone and dialed Tate's private number.

*****

Phoebe was on the back patio, hardly daring to believe that she had moved out of Flatbush Scheme. Here, there was no pig scent or unsightly ceilings. Here was a simple elegance and she even heard birds chirping. She closed her eyes and propped up her foot on the balcony rail.

She had packed out her meager possessions in the back room. It was the room Erica said was the coolest, and the one she had been living in up until recently. Phoebe had promptly headed for it. Her old bedroom could fit in there at least three times. There was something to be said for living comfortably.

She leaned back in the lounge chair. The portable radio was turned down really low and she was humming to the songs. Her phone rang and she glanced at the screen—Charles. How fitting she was just thinking about him.

"Phoebe what does your mother mean by you've moved out?"

Phoebe grinned. "Hello to you too. Yes I moved out."

"Are you living with your rich guy?" Charles asked panicking. "I just need a couple of years Phoebe. I can provide for you."

Phoebe laughed, "Charles Black, I am not living with anybody. I am house sitting at Kelly's house, the same place we had dinner with Erica and Caleb."

"Oh," Charles said, relieved. "So who am I to play Scrabble with tonight, now that you are gone?"

Phoebe laughed. "You are cordially invited to my new place tonight to play Scrabble." She gave him directions.

"Okay, see you later." Charles hung up the phone and Phoebe went back to her music. She liked Charles a lot and he was a fabulous kisser, but did she want to spend the rest of her life with him?

Her mind was telling her no. As much as Charles was fun to be around, she was not really the outgoing social butterfly type. She was more like Ezekiel in personality, she knew somebody who would be perfect for Charles though.

She dialed Tanya's number.

"Charles is coming to play Scrabble with me tonight. You want to meet him?"

"Oh yes," Tanya said eagerly. "What should I bring?"

"Yourself." Phoebe laughed.

*****

Phoebe heard Charles coming from all the way down the end of the road; his car made a spluttering sound then stopped. She turned on the outside lights and peered outside the window. Charles was with his sister Pinky.

Phoebe smiled when she opened the door. She liked Pinky. She had an easy way about her, almost like her brother.

"Hey." Charles greeted Phoebe. He was handsomely dressed in all black. "She is spending the week with me; apparently she was fired from her job today."

Pinky growled, "Hi Phoebe. Your friend Chris Donahue is the most infuriating man on the entire planet."

"Come on in," Phoebe murmured. "Correction though, last I checked, Chris was not my friend."

"All I did," Pinky fumed walking in, "was ask him why is he still so hung up on Kelly Palmer? That's all. The man actually told me that I passed my place and gave me the boot."

"From the hotel?" Phoebe asked curiously. "I set up the Scrabble in the kitchen, come this way."

They followed Phoebe.

"No," Pinky said still miffed. "The original receptionist came back for her job and he offered me a job at his Bluffs Head mansion as a housekeeper. I get time off for school and the pay was good so I said yes. But he is so strung out on Kelly that I told him to get a grip. He fired me because of that."

She threw up her hand in the air. "I probably shouldn't even be telling you this. I signed a confidentiality agreement that I would not discuss him with anyone for up to three years after my employment terminated. But he already booted me. What can he do now, huh? Send me to gossiper's prison."

Phoebe looked at her as she sat in a huff on the chair surrounding the table. She admired Pinky's long multicolored dress that hugged her petite figure, and her blond hair that sported a spiky hair cut that was brushed to the front, and smirked, "you are the prettiest housekeeper I have ever seen."

Pinky rolled her eyes. "So?"

"So, maybe Chris Donahue is getting over Kelly and not handling it well. Just saying."

Charles groaned. "All I've been hearing since she got home is how evil Chris Donahue is. Can we talk about something else?"

"Well we could talk about the fact that this is Kelly's house," Phoebe said looking at Pinky closely.

"It is?" Pinky said wonderingly. "Can I look around?"

"She didn't leave any pictures or anything like that lying around," Phoebe said grinning at Pinky. "Somebody likes their boss and is curious about his lady love."

Pinky bit her lip. "Okay, we really need to change the topic."

The doorbell rang at the same time and Phoebe went to answer it.

It was Tanya. She had her sister locks out, and they were almost to her waist. She was wearing a summer dress with bird patterns all over it.

"You look pretty," Phoebe said, "and your hair has grown. I never noticed how long it was before."

"Where is he?" Tanya asked eagerly.

"My guests have no manners." Phoebe ushered her into the kitchen. "Tanya Smart, meet Charles and Pinky Black."

"Oh four of us for Scrabble," Charles said grinning at Tanya. "This will be fun."

And it was fun. Pinky played snarky words and called Chris every one she could think of.

Charles kept on asking Tanya questions about herself and when he found out that she loved to sing he invited her to his band practice.

"We are looking for a female lead," he said, "maybe you can come and show us what you got."

Phoebe looked at them. When they started talking, she and Pinky were all but invisible.

This was probably how it should be. She felt a faint wrench when she thought about Charles and Tanya, but then she convinced herself that she was happier being single anyway.

Chapter Twenty-Four

One month after Phoebe moved into Kelly's house, she felt pleased with herself. She had a system going on that was truly working. Tanya picked her up in the morning to go to work and Erica picked her up to go to church.

So what if she felt lonely at the oddest times, like on Wednesday when she was having lunch with Tanya and she was gushing over Charles and his friends and how great a time they were having?

On Thursday when Charles called to tell her, with a besotted tone in his voice, that he thought Tanya was a great girl, or on Friday when out of sheer loneliness she called Ezekiel's phone and his assistant answered saying he was indisposed.

Phoebe was especially depressed at that; she had never really missed Ezekiel until he left her completely alone.

She sighed when she got home on Friday evening. There was a big open weekend in front of her, but there was no one to spend it with.

She jumped when her phone rang and picked it up dejectedly. The ID on the phone said private number.

"Hello," she answered gingerly—she hated taking calls from private numbers.

"Phoebe." His voice was smooth and smoky.

"Ezekiel," Phoebe whispered feeling excited and trembly all at the same time.

"Sounds like you missed me," he chuckled

"I actually do," Phoebe said a big grin on her face. "I know we are no longer together, but I hadn't heard from you in sooo long that I thought you had forgotten me."

"No I haven't. I'll never forget you."

Phoebe flushed at that. "I'll never forget you either."

"I am in Switzerland," Ezekiel's voice sounded smooth as honey, "I had something to take care of. I will probably be here for six months or more."

That was the start of their daily phone calls; they spoke everyday, sometimes for hours.

Phoebe found herself rushing to go home and do her chores so that she could be free for the nightly calls.

It had become such an obsession for her that she kept looking at her watch while she was hanging out with Erica and Tanya after church.

"Why are you looking at your watch so eagerly?" Erica asked her for the fourth time.

"It's nothing." Phoebe grinned secretly.

"Now listen, Missy," Erica said, "you know I can't stand a secret. What is going on?"

Phoebe giggled. "It's just that I've been talking to Ezekiel every night for the past couple of weeks. I want to go home and freshen up and get into bed before he calls. I especially like when all the lights are off and there's just the two of us in the dark."

Tanya's eyes widened. "Are you serious? You back with Ezekiel Hoppings?"

Phoebe smirked. "I don't know. We just talk. We talk about everything and nothing. I even have him listening to music with me over the phone. I can't explain it; he's become like a good friend. You know," she blushed, and her ears turned red, "you know."

Erica clapped her hand over her mouth, "I can't believe it! Do you love him?"

Phoebe wailed, "I don't know. I think I am addicted to him, like one would be addicted to a radio program. You know you can't get enough of it and you eagerly wait for the next hit."

"She loves him," Tanya said dryly. "She loves her ugly, rich guy."

"Can we leave yet?" Phoebe asked. "Who is dropping me home?"

"I will," Tanya said. "I am going down to Vanley's Bar with The Perfect Number. I was going to ask you if you want to come."

"No thanks," Phoebe said impatiently.

"Can you tear yourself away from Ezekiel on Thursday next week and come to my house for dinner?" Erica asked, "You too Tanya, and bring Charles. It's Caleb's birthday. It will be a nice little party; I invited some of his friends from work along with you guys."

"Sure," Phoebe said, "I'll be there. Charles hardly calls me anymore, Tanya might be the reason."

Tanya got into her car blushing. "Ah the complexities of life and love."

Erica grinned. "See y'all next Thursday."

*****

Chris Donahue was at Caleb's party and was standing by himself in a corner beside a bookcase cradling a cup of drinks when Phoebe arrived with Tanya. Caleb's friends were a fun bunch to be around and she was soon involved in a conversation when Chris came and sat beside her. His hazel eyes were more green than brown at the moment and he had a far away look in his eye.

"Are you sure you want to sit beside me?" Phoebe asked him when the group had drifted off for more cake. "I might hound you to marry me?"

Chris looked at her contemplatively. "I never understood that whole stalking thing you did. You were doing it like a woman possessed." He grinned. "Like you had a list or something. One day I swear I saw you rifling through my garbage bin at home."

"I had no idea where you lived until the other day I went to Bluffs Head," Phoebe said smiling. "Besides garbage bins are not my thing. I am sorry about that whole episode. I did have a list. My mother had a ten-point plan to catch you. I didn't even really like you like that."

Chris guffawed. "I am sorry too for embarrassing you like that before the entire church. It's just that I couldn't seem to shake you."

Phoebe shrugged. "I deserved it. No woman in her right mind should have been so thirsty. I am happy I am back to my senses once more."

Chris looked at her contemplatively. "So, is Charles Black your boyfriend?"

"Nope," Phoebe said, "I am single."

Chris shook his head. "What about Ezekiel?"

Phoebe blushed. "He's great! But no we aren't together."

"Ah," Chris took a sip of his drink, "I saw a pause there when I mentioned Ezekiel. He told me you refused to marry him because of your integrity. I'm happy for you Phoebe."

Phoebe flushed. "I belatedly found my principles and shook that particular demon off my back. What about you?" Phoebe asked.

"Still here alone." Chris said forlornly.

"Cheer up," Phoebe said. "Take it from your former stalker; you are a good catch for one lucky woman."

Chris looked at her warmly. "You know Phoebe, you are not too bad."

Phoebe grinned. "You are not too bad yourself."

The mood was broken when Charles came and sat beside Phoebe on the other side.

"Want to dance?"

"Sure," Phoebe said joining the young people on the floor.

They were dancing to some old reggae tunes. Phoebe laughed at Charles' antics, he was gyrating and making crazy faces, and the other dancers were cheering him on.

"I hardly see you these days, what are you up to?" They danced to the balcony and Phoebe leaned on the rails, inhaling the night air.

Charles looked at Phoebe. "I've been spending lots of time practicing with the band."

"And hanging out with the new female singer," Phoebe prompted gently.

"I don't know how it happened," Charles said painfully, "but one moment I was so hotly in love with you and the next thing I know, I was in love with Tanya. But it's not the same. With her, it's different. It's like we move to the same beat." He looked down at the ground sheepishly. "I feel like such a dog."

Phoebe laughed. "Promise me one thing."

"What?" Charles asked eagerly,

"Don't you stop your plans to improve, and never stop

living life simply. It's nice to find someone with whom you move to the same beat, huh?"

Charles smiled in relief. "It is," then he knitted his brow. "You are taking this well. I thought you and I had a thing going on, especially after you ditched Ezekiel Hoppings."

"I liked kissing you," Phoebe said blushing. "Okay, I really enjoyed it, but I didn't see us moving to the same beat, you understand?"

Charles nodded. "Perfectly. It's a relief to get that cleared up, because I want to kiss Tanya, and I was feeling a tad bit guilty about you. I can stop torturing myself now."

Phoebe smiled. "Well you have my blessing. I introduced you two on purpose, by the way. Tanya really wanted to meet you."

"Is that so?" Charles asked, a pleased look on his face. "Wait...does this mean that we can't play Scrabble together again?"

"Oh no," Phoebe wagged her finger at him, "come over any day you have some free time. Call before you come by though."

*****

When Phoebe got in that night, her phone rang at eleven thirty.

"How was the party?" It was Ezekiel. His smooth honey voice was enough to make her heart pick up speed.

She gave him a run down, and as usual they conversed for long minutes.

Phoebe finally acknowledged to herself when he hung up the phone that she wasn't merely addicted to Ezekiel Hoppings' voice, she loved him.

Admitting it to herself was giving her quite the shock. She

sat on the bed and contemplated it.

It definitely was not one of those love at first sight situations because Ezekiel was not handsome. It wasn't even the fact that he was rich, she had gotten past that whole rich handsome guy thing.

She loved him because they were friends. She could tell him anything, even those deep dark secrets about herself that she thought were terrible.

Like the fact that she was reared to be a gold-digger, and the fact that she stalked Chris Donahue for two long months, and how she would approach men to find out what kind of car they drove. He heard her out and didn't judge.

He even shared his secrets with her too, like the fact that he was afraid of plastic surgery because of his two-year stay in hospital when the doctor's thought he would die, and that he became a Christian because during his stay, at the hospital, he dreamt of a kindly man who kept telling him that Jesus was waiting to get to know him.

She wished fervently that she could see him and tell him to his dear battered face that she loved him.

It was a wondrous feeling, this love thing; she curled up in her bed and tried to analyze it. It wasn't just physical attraction though. That kiss that they shared at his dinner kept replaying in her mind.

Indeed it had taken up a good part of thoughts lately. She wanted more kisses from him, and it didn't matter how he looked, or that he had scars. She just wanted him near. She wished he'd hurry up with his business in Switzerland so that she could tell him face to face that she loved him.

Chapter Twenty-Five

Ezekiel always played to win and during the six months he spent in Switzerland he made sure that he kept Phoebe close by telephone. He had racked up quite a phone bill from the private facility in which he stayed while he recuperated from surgery.

He hadn't seen her for seven whole months and his longing to see her, to touch her was intense.

A few months ago he would have looked in the mirror at the stranger looking back at him and fretfully wondered if he had made the right decision. His business acquaintances wouldn't recognize him now.

Even his assistant Nathan had been shocked at his transformation. Ezekiel had gotten over the urge, a few weeks earlier, of constantly touching his jaw to feel the smoothness of his skin.

Neville Tate had even removed the stains from his teeth. He had wanted to go to Jamaica as soon as his transformation was complete, but Nathan had insisted that they take his face out on a test drive.

They went to a cafe and the response to him was overwhelmingly good. Women who would not give him a second glance before had actually smiled at him and given him coquettish looks under their eyelashes. It was ego boosting and only made him want to go to Jamaica even more.

He sat in Nathan's office waiting for him to stop prodding and cooing over his face.

"Yup, you are fit to leave," Nathan said proudly, "I declare your cosmetic procedures to be successful. You are such a handsome fella."

"Thanks," Ezekiel said gruffly. "Now I need to go home and see my girl."

Nathan laughed. "She won't recognize you from the battered face I had to sort out."

Ezekiel thought about that all the way to Jamaica. How would he do this? For all the time he was at the clinic, he never told Phoebe what he was doing. How should he approach this?

*****

Phoebe was tidying her desk to go to lunch; a slight feeling of depression had dogged her all week. It seemed as if everybody's life was moving on and falling into place nicely.

Erica was planning for her baby's arrival in one month, and all she did was talk baby talk; she made a note to herself, if she was ever blessed to conceive a child, she wouldn't bore people to tears about every little development of her fetus like Erica did.

Tanya was so involved with her newly found music career

and her involvement with Charles that she hardly saw either of them.

Even her mother was scarce these days; she'd called Ezekiel's aunt at his suggestion and gotten her a job as a house-mother in the new place of safety for children they had setup for abused children. Apparently Nishta had taken to it like a duck to water. She had several children under her care and she was beginning to realize that their kind of poor was not that bad. There were persons who were much worse off than she could even think. These days Nishta was extremely subdued.

Phoebe wished Ezekiel was around; just speaking to him on the phone wasn't enough any longer and she wished that she hadn't broken up with him. She wished she had somebody to do buddy stuff with. But here she was, back to square one.

At least this time her unhappiness wasn't borne out of covetousness. This time she was unhappy because she felt lonely. A deep sort of loneliness that only the person you loved could fill.

She sighed loudly.

"That is a loud sigh," Vanessa popped her head over the cubicle, "feeling down?"

Phoebe had made nice with her fellow colleagues for the past few months and they had been surprisingly responsive. She now realized that the old adage 'he who wants friends must show himself friendly' was right.

She nodded wanly at Vanessa.

Vanessa whispered conspiratorially, "If you see the dishy guy that Mr. King was ushering into his office and genuflecting to, you would cheer up."

"Oh my gosh, here he comes, tall, caramel, handsome." She hunkered back down around her desk.

"I'm not interested." Phoebe murmured limply. "I would

take battered face, sexy voice and cares for me any day over some slick rich guy that's out for a good time."

"Miss Bridge!" Mr. King was standing behind her. When Phoebe spun around he had a look of wonder in his eyes. "I would like to introduce you to the chief shareholder of the bank."

Phoebe looked at the man beside Mr. King, her eyes flickering in surprise. Why did he want to be introduced to her? She was just junior staff.

He smiled at her slowly and then he cleared his throat. "Actually, I wanted to ask you to lunch at the Villa Rose... heard that the chef, Caleb Wright, does some excellent food."

All ears were perked up around the surrounding cubicles and Vanessa's head popped up sharply at that.

Phoebe smiled. "Well er, sir..." There was something disturbingly familiar about his voice and his perfume.

She looked at him closely and then it suddenly dawned on her that it was Ezekiel.

How on earth could it be him though? His features were asymmetrical, even perfect, not a scar in sight, but who could mistake those eyes and those curling eyelashes and that body.

"That's why you went to Switzerland?" she squealed, running into his arms, almost trampling Mr. King.

She hugged him tight and he gripped her even tighter.

"I missed you so bad," she mumbled in his jacket.

"I missed you too," he whispered in her hair.

He looked over her head at Mr. King. "I am afraid I am going to have to fire her."

Mr. King had still not recovered from Phoebe's squeal of delight and mad dash toward Mr. Hoppings. "Oh well, Sir, may I ask why?"

Phoebe was giggling and trying to burrow herself even

closer to him.

"I am going to marry her," Ezekiel said solemnly, "and I want her with me when I travel. Her attendance record would be atrocious if she stayed here."

Mr. King nodded in dazed understanding.

He walked Phoebe through the bank, with her stunned co-workers looking on in disbelief.

When they reached his car, Phoebe hung onto Ezekiel like a limpet.

"You look gorgeous," she said staring at him avidly. "My gosh, we are no longer beauty and the beast anymore are we?" She asked drinking him in.

"No," Ezekiel chuckled, "now both of us are beautiful together."

"I had no idea you'd do this." Phoebe touched his cheek once again. "Your scars are all gone, just when I was gearing up to tell you that I love you, scars and all, and beg you to come home."

Ezekiel chuckled and then stared at her seriously. "It took your selfless decision to be good inside and to reconcile your attitude and motivations to God to make me overcome the fear I had of doing the procedures."

He twisted around in the drivers seat and held her hand. "I am so proud of your decision to be independent and to find yourself without a man's validation, but I'm afraid I'm going to have to ask you to re-think that position, Phoebe Bridge. I'm a rich man, there's nothing much I can do about that, I can scale down my businesses and I am doing that but I'll always be wealthy. Despite this handicap, will you marry me?"

Phoebe stared at him and then laughed. "Of course I'll marry you. I'll be more than happy to pledge to love, honor and cherish you as long as we both shall live, with the utmost honesty, before God and man."

He kissed her deeply. "Remember when you said that your friend Erica told you that if we got married it would be unholy matrimony?"

Phoebe nodded.

"Well, that won't be true now, will it?"

Phoebe shook her head. "I love you Ezekiel. I loved you even when you were ugly on the outside."

Ezekiel touched her cheek tenderly, "and I, I loved you even more when you discovered your true beauty within."

THE END

Here's an excerpt from- If It Aint Broke (Chris' Story/ Three Rivers Series Book 4)

Chris eagerly sorted through the mail that was arranged neatly on the desk in his study. Today was Thursday, the day he gets his weekly updates from his P.I. in Cayman. His hands hovered the manila envelope and then put it aside for last.

He had other mail too. His eye caught a gold envelope with fancy lettering on the front. He picked it up contemplatively and sniffed the air; it smelled really sweet, like roses.

He opened it and saw an impressive invitation, Chris Donahue and Guest: you are cordially invited to the nuptials of Ezekiel Abbas Hoppings and Phoebe Amita Bridge on Sunday, December 8 at the Lion's Gate Estate, Grand Cayman.

A tremor raced through Chris' when he read the words Cayman and then he spared a thought for Phoebe and Ezekiel—he was happy for them. He had seen his friend and neighbor recently. He had looked so different and relaxed and extremely happy.

He ran his fingers through his hair and got up from the chair he had been sitting in.

It was as if a fat fist was cutting off his air when he thought of Cayman—he wondered if Ezekiel invited the Palmers. Wasn't he friends with Kelly?

After nearly three years, would he be seeing Kelly face to face at this particular wedding?

And what if they brought his son? Was he supposed to act as if he didn't care when he saw him?

He would decline this invitation. He couldn't go through with it. He had declined the invitation to go to Erica and Caleb's wedding. That one had been too close to home.

And who were they expecting him to carry anyway, he hadn't dated anyone since that disastrous few months with that clingy girl, Estella.

His mouth tightened in pain. His life so far had been work, work and more work. He had more money now than he had ever had, but he was left with the cold dregs of unrequited love for a married woman who had his only child and was living happily with her husband in Cayman.

He lifted the brown envelope almost reluctantly, he would be in a bad mood after this; he wished his housekeeper wasn't around with her nosy concern. There was something about Pinky Black that made him angry too. She was defiant and nosy and didn't know the meaning of subservience. Her bright, perkiness annoyed him. He had fired her twice before, and everyday since rehiring her he has thought about firing her again.

He looked at the envelope again, he was stalling and for good reason. He always felt like a dirty voyeur who was punishing himself unnecessarily with the pictures he commissioned the detective to take of his young son and his mother. He had only started having them trailed and pictures taken of them after finding himself in an extremely dark place on his son's first birthday.

Why should he just step back from his child's life? He needed to know how he was getting on. That the knowing was also a punishment for him didn't matter.

He opened the envelope and there they were, a picture of Kelly and Mark walking on the beach. Kelly was in a sky blue maxi dress and his son was in swimming trunks with a bucket in hand.

He had grown taller, taller than he looked in last week's picture. His hair was longer too, almost like a girl's, and curly. Mark's little cherubic cheeks had a dimple and Chris felt his and again realized that his son was a miniature copy of himself.

Kelly was looking slimmer and toned and he wondered if she was working out. He heaved a sigh, forcefully slammed down the thoughts of her from his mind and put the pictures back into the envelope.

He still held on to them though as his mind tortured him about the two of them. Usually he read the detective's report but these days it was getting repetitive.

Last week Kelly took him to a kiddies' attraction, the week before that he had a cold. His heart had throbbed uncomfortably until the detective reported that he was well again.

He loved his child. He wanted him. Not because of some selfish desire to break up their family but because the boy was his—his first born, and why was he the only one punished for that ill-fated affair?

He sighed, a big tremulous sigh that did nothing to loosen the tight fist that had taken permanent residence around his heart, and locked the manila envelope, along with its contents, into a bottom draw of his desk.

He was thinking that he would frame some of the pictures to track the development of his child. Then again maybe not, that would mean that everyday would be Thursday for him.

He heard a soft knocking on his study door, and he contemplated ignoring it, but knowing Pinky she would barge right in and bulldoze him with her overwhelming personality after trying the soft approach.

"Come in," he said gruffly, bracing himself for his unconventional housekeeper.

Pinky popped her head around the door. "Hey boss man, I've got drama class tonight. Won't be around, ya dig?" She was chewing a gum as if she was going to murder it.

Chris sighed, "Pinky, how many times must I ask you not to refer to me as boss man."

"Four hundred and ninety," was the facetious reply. "I started counting it on my phone." She came fully into the study and Chris inhaled sharply. "What on earth do you have on?"

Pinky looked down at herself. She was in very tight bike shorts and a red halter neck blouse. "Do I look dangerous?" She purred and swayed her hips while walking up to Chris' desk.

OTHER BOOKS BY BRENDA BARRETT

Contemporary Romance

Loving Mr. Wright (Three Rivers Series) - A man with a past. A woman who was tired of being single. Erica was tired of searching for the right man, she had all but resigned herself to a single life but then the mysterious Caleb Wright showed up and Erica saw one last opportunity to ditch her single life. He was perfect for her. But what was he hiding? Could his past be that bad that they could not get pass it?

Private Sins (Three Rivers Series- Book One)- Kelly was in deep trouble, her husband was a pastor and she his loyal first lady. Well she was…until she had an affair with Chris; the first elder of their church. And now she was pregnant with his child. Could she keep the secret from her husband and pretend that all was well? Or should she confess her private sin and let the chips fall where they may?

The Preacher And The Prostitute - Prostitution and the clergy don't mix. Tell that to ex-prostitute Maribel who finds herself in love with the Pastor at her church. Can an ex-prostitute and a pastor have a future together?

New Beginnings - When self-styled 'ghetto queen', Geneva, was contacted by lawyers who claimed that Stanley Walters, the deceased uptown financier, was her father she was told that his will stipulated that she had to live with her sister uptown to forge sisterly bonds. Leaving Froggie, her 'ghetto don', behind she found herself battling with Pamela her stepmother and battling her emotions for Justin a suave up-towner.

Full Circle - After Diana graduated from school, she had a couple of things to do, returning to Jamaica to find her siblings was top priority. Additionally, she needed to take a well-earned vacation. What she didn't foresee was that she would meet Robert Cassidy and that both their pasts would be so intertwined that disturbing questions would pop up about their parentage, just when they were getting close.

Love Triangle - There are always three sides to a story when there is a love triangle, the why's and the how's are best answered when the individuals involved tell the stories through their eyes and experiences.

Historical Fiction/Romance

The Empty Hammock - Workaholic, Ana Mendez, was certain that her mother was getting senile, when she said she found a treasure chest in the back yard. After unsuccessfully trying to open the old treasure chest, Ana fell asleep in a hammock, and woke up in the year 1494 in Jamaica! It was the time of the Tainos, a time when life seemed simpler, but Ana knew that all of that was about to change.

The Pull Of Freedom - Even in bondage the people freshly arrived from Africa considered themselves free. Led by Nanny and Cudjoe the slaves escaped the Simmonds' plantation and went in different directions to forge their destiny in the new country called Jamaica.

Jamaican Comedy (Material contains Jamaican dialect)

Di Taxi Ride And Other Stories - Di Taxi Ride and Other Stories is a collection of twelve witty and fast paced short

CPSIA information can be obtained at www.ICGtesting.com
Printed in the USA
LVOW07s2340230914

405525LV00014B/87/P